Ben Nelson

Defender of the Faithful

by Ted Linder

Ben Nelson

Defender of the Faithful

by Ted Linder

HERALD PUBLISHING HOUSE
Independence, Missouri

Library of Congress Cataloging in Publication Data

Linder, Ted.
  Ben Nelson, defender of the faithful.

  1. Nelson, Ben.   2. Mormons—United States—
Biography. I. Title.
BX8695.N37L56   289.3′3 [B]   81-7190
ISBN 0-8309-0321-6   AACR2

Printed in the United States of America

This book is dedicated to my grandchildren and my great-grandchildren whom I probably will never see but already love because they will be mine.

Ted Linder

Preface

This book is about young Ben Nelson who, during the early 1830s, dares to defend his "Mormon" friends. There are fast rides, fistfights, and the facing of great odds.

The historical events are true, although the time sequence is altered. Some happenings that took several days have been compacted into one so events move more quickly.

Ben's relationship with his stepfather is not a close one until they face danger together; then they develop strong ties of loyalty. There is capture of his friend Phillip Farris and the blossoming of romance with Phil's sister Alice. There is his race to warn the Farris family of impending danger. In all ways Ben proves himself a man although he is only seventeen when the story begins.

Chapter 1

Ben Nelson was glad that his stepfather, Wesley Bradford, had hired Indian George to help him break the horses. George had taught him how to gentle-break a horse, and this was what Wes wanted. While some had been ridden, this last batch was wild. Wes had got them from some Osage Indians who had brought them to Independence to trade for blankets and other "white man's" articles. They also wanted whiskey, but Wes drew the line there. They had to get their liquor elsewhere.

Ben's two sisters, Becky and Flo, both younger than he, came out to watch the "fun" as they called it. Though he had just turned seventeen, Ben had reached a stage of muscularity equal to an older man. Working with horses, stalking game in the forest, and helping Fred, the Negro slave, on the farm had made his muscles like whipcords. Ben and the Indian went into the corral and cornered a beautiful bay mare which snorted and pranced nervously as they approached. Ben enlarged the loop in his rope, gave it a throw, and missed. The second time was better. Digging his heels into the dirt, he held on while the mare fought against the rope until she began to choke. He always hated this part, but the horse had to submit to his handling. Now he took a turn around the snubbing post. George walked up to the animal and started talking to it. Wes always said that the Indian could speak horse language, but this time the mare tried to pull away. His sisters yelled in protest that they were hurting her. His mother, Caroline—a good horsewoman herself—came out to assist. George grabbed the rope and tightened it about the twitching neck. Out of breath, the mare lay down, and George quickly hobbled her front feet. Then Ben loosened the rope so she could breathe better.

"Let her smell you now. You are the one who will be riding her," George said. "Blow your breath in her nostrils."

Ben held the mare's head and blew his breath in her nose. The animal was coming around. He called, "Mama, come here and let her get used to you. She'll make you a good riding horse."

Caroline opened the gate, closed it, and approached the animal. She talked in a soothing voice, rubbed its head, and blew her breath in its nostrils. This pleased the Indian. This was his way. "Now she will like you," he told Mrs. Bradford.

The mare quivered a little as George rubbed a blanket along her back. Then keeping the hobbles on her, they let her up. She was breathing easier. Ben wondered how much training she had already received from her Indian owners—obviously she was not completely wild. George kept up his horse talk while Caroline rubbed and soothed her. Then the Indian took the blanket, let her smell it, and threw it on her back. They all stepped back as George held onto the rope. As the mare stood there, muscles twitching, Ben walked over to the fence and got a saddle. He let her smell it, then placed it over the blanket on her back. Forming a hackamore around her nose and head, he stooped down and freed her from the hobbles while George held her head in a strong grip. She started to fight, so they snubbed her close to the post. Ben tightened the saddle cinch. Now was the test.

Would she try to throw him? He had been thrown before. Grabbing the loose ends of the hackamore, he vaulted into the saddle. George, who had been holding her head, turned her loose. She stood there for a moment with her head down. Ben pulled her head around to the left to keep her from bucking, if that was on her mind. She started to rare on her hind legs, and then trotted peacefully around the enclosure. George opened the gate and Ben took her for a good run in the pasture. She had been ridden before, but he did not know what treatment she had had. She responded well. Neck reining her, he put her through her paces, then brought her back to his mother who had been watching near the pasture gate. Rubbing the mare's face with her hands, Caroline let her smell her breath. George held the horse's head as Ben jumped down. His mother mounted, hooking her knee over the horn sidesaddle fashion. The mare whinnied but responded to Caroline's promptings and headed for the pasture. Caroline shamelessly put her leg over the horse and rode "man style" with both feet in the stirrups. She was an excellent rider. The bay mare responded to her so well that when she rode up to the little group that had been watching her she was flushed of face and her eyes were shining. Carefully gathering her skirts around her, she dismounted in the corral after her daughters had opened the gate for her. Flo hugged her, and Becky exclaimed, "You looked beautiful, Mama. I wish I could ride that well."

"Me too," Flo said. "I hope Papa won't sell her. She will make you and me and Becky a good riding horse."

Ben beamed at his mother. He was proud of her skill as a horsewoman. It was too bad that Wes had not been there to witness that beautiful ride. George grunted, "Your mama rides like Indian," and Ben knew that was a compliment.

The bay mare did become Caroline's, although others in the family were allowed to ride her. The horse acknowledged this ownership; and if Caroline went into the pasture the mare—named Kitten—would follow her. Wes noticed this and, when he was in one of his bad moods, would threaten to sell her. At such times the whole family would turn on him, and he would beat a hasty retreat to other parts of the house or farm. Ben had his own mount, a buckskin named Comanche, and Wes had a blooded horse from the East. The girls could ride whatever was safe and available at the time. Ben's buckskin was tough and could be ridden all day without tiring. Ben had trained him for the hunt, so he was not gun-shy. Often when he first mounted of a morning the horse would want to run, and Ben usually let him get it out of his system.

These horses that Wes brought in from buying jaunts around the country and purchased from the Osages had to be broken before they could be sold. Sometimes Wes helped, but he usually had George and Ben do the job. Some turned out good for riding; others made buggy or plow horses. It was mostly up to Ben to judge. Wes and his stepson quarreled a bit, but he knew Ben did his work well.

There was a slave couple on the farm. Fred took care of the field, with Ben's help, and his wife Blanche took care of the house. Although he had jobs he was expected to do, Ben also had a lot of free time to hunt and explore the forests and prairies.

Wes was given to drinking and gambling, but he was a good provider. With his ready wit and charm and big-framed body that forewarned any would-be trouble-makers to keep their distance, he was generally well-liked and respected in the community. He traded horses, and he made money. Ben sometimes had open quarrels with him, but he usually tried to avoid them for his mother's sake.

Ben and George spent a couple of weeks or more working with the band of horses until they were so tame that Flo and Becky could handle most of them. Wes wanted them gentle-broke—not just broken. Any hard-riding man could break a horse, but gentle-breaking took a special kind of skill and patience. Sometimes a neighbor brought a horse to Ben for this pur-pose—which added a little more money to his savings. He had in mind that one day he would join the trappers who traveled up the Missouri River every year.

One day while Ben and George were breaking horses he saw several ox-drawn wagons going down the road past the farm to the west. He went into the house and called his mother's attention to the caravan. She watched from the porch as the wagons disappeared around a bend in the road.

"Must be those Mormons Wes spoke about," she said.

"You mean the people who run the print shop in Independence?"

"Yes."

"One of them has a blacksmith shop, too. I took some of the horses there to be shod."

"They have a store also. . .and a settlement on Big Blue River. Looks as if these travelers might be headed

13

there. I think Wes will be pleased that they are not stopping here . . . although the ones we've met seem honest and upright."

"Mama, why do you knuckle down to Papa? Sometimes I think you let him run over you."

"Well, son, when you were small and your father was killed in a flood, Wes came along and was good to us. He wasn't always cross and hard to get along with. In fact he was quite the opposite. Then, after your sisters were born, he got to drinking and gambling. I really don't know what made him change, but something happened. He still does a lot of kind things, but I'll admit he's sometimes hard on you. I'm sorry about that; however, you are almost grown and will soon be out on your own. He has let you have the run of the place without much supervision, and this has given you lots of self-assurance. Someday I hope we can find out what is wrong with him . . . then maybe we can help. Until then I can put up with him . . . if you can."

When Wes came home that evening his face was flushed. He walked stiffly from the corral where he had left his horse still saddled and ordered Ben to go tend to it. Then he went into the bedroom to sleep off the effect of his drinking. The family was relieved.

Ben went out to the corral, unsaddled the horse, and gave him some oats. The horse looked around as if to say thanks as Ben curried him and put him in his stall. Returning to the house, Ben could hear Wes snoring in the bedroom. He went out on the porch, where his mother and sisters joined him. The quietness of the evening settled upon them, and they felt at peace with the world.

At the same time to the west on the Big Blue River a group of weary people were unyoking travel-weary oxen at the settlement there. They called themselves "Saints," but the townspeople called them "Mormons." They made some strange claims that bothered those who had already settled in the area. They believed that this was their chosen land, and that their purpose in life was to create a condition that would herald the second coming of Jesus. They believed they were divinely commissioned to set up his church in the last days.

As Ben sat on the steps of the porch enjoying the pleasant presence of his mother and sisters, he thought of the trappers who had camped on the Missouri River not far away. How he would like to be a part of that group of men who went to the mountains to trap all winter! In no way did he consider a future with the group of pilgrims who had driven their ox teams by that day.

Chapter 2

As he sat on his horse, Comanche, Ben heard the sound of an ax shattering the quietness of the forest. With his rifle across the saddle he headed for the sound. Soon he heard voices singing to the cadence of the ax blows—a man's deep bass and a woman's soprano. There there was a burst of laughter. He had just had an argument with Wes, and it was hard for him to see how anyone could be that happy. Maybe he should join one of the groups of trappers heading up the Missouri River almost daily now. Most of them stopped in Independence to do some trading and to get drunk one more time before hitting the wilds. The more he thought about his stepfather, the more appealing this idea for escape became. He would save all he could for supplies and traps. Maybe when he was eighteen . . . that would be a good age to make the break. He was tall, and he could handle most of the boys in the neighborhood in a tussle. Wes had taken time to show him some of the rough and tumble ways of fighting, and he was a good teacher since he often got into brawls himself when he was drinking.

Ben caught sight of a clearing in the timber and approached what seemed to be a camp. A brush shelter had been thrown up, and a covered wagon stood nearby. A man and a boy about his own age were working on some logs that had been dragged up, apparently by a team of oxen that were chewing their cuds nearby. A woman about his mother's age was cooking at a makeshift fireplace. A girl in her early teens was helping her. The girl must have said something funny, and they both

16

laughed. Ben sat quietly and watched. It was a pretty sight . . . a pretty sight indeed, he thought. The boy had dark hair and was well tanned—like the father. The girl was a young duplicate of her mother—willowy, fair-haired. Ben could not tell from his distance, but he bet she had blue eyes.

Swinging down from the saddle and cradling his rifle in his arm, he led his horse to the clearing. All activities stopped as he approached, and the suddenly grave-faced family looked him over from head to toe. Then the father smiled and spoke. "Come in . . . come in. Welcome to our humble abode."

Ben tied Comanche to a bush, leaned his rifle against a tree, and moved toward the now smiling group.

"You are entering our kitchen and our living room and sometimes bedroom," the family laughed at the father's humor. He took Ben's hand in a warm hand-shake. "I am Jack Farris. Who might you be, sir?"

"Ben Nelson, sir."

"This is my son, Phillip . . . my wife, Virginia . . . and this little shy one is my daughter, Alice. She took all the good looks away from Phillip and me. Of course her mother shared hers with her."

Alice blushed as she took Ben's hand. Her eyes *were* blue—deep blue.

"Are you one of our neighbors?" Jack Farris asked.

"Yes, I live on a farm just a little way east of here . . . near Independence. I usually hunt in here and was surprised to see a house going up."

"Yes we were fortunate to get this close to town. Many of our friends went farther west in the county—government land, you know. The group we are with came from New York and Ohio. We are trying to 'wrest a home from the wilderness,' as the saying goes. We would offer you a chair but we seem to be out of that item. Would you sit here on a log with my son and me? Mother, would you bring out your fine china? We have our first guest in our new home, and we would like him to dine with us. You will, won't you?"

Ben agreed and seated himself on the log next to Phillip. The women busied themselves around the fire. Phillip was eager to know about hunting in the area. Ben told him that it had been very good with plenty of deer and wild turkey. Then Phillip wanted to examine Ben's gun. Ben retrieved it from where he had put it. Phillip's eyes glowed as he sighted down it and rubbed his hands over it.

Ben asked, "Do you have a rifle?"

"No, but I will as soon as I can pay for one."

"If you want, I'll bring over an extra one, and we'll go for a hunt."

"That would be great! I had an uncle who taught me how to shoot. I went with him sometimes."

"Do you ride?"

"I'll say I do, but I lost my pony. He died on the way out here."

"I'll bring one over for you sometime, and we'll go riding. We sell and trade horses. Usually we have several, but at times we don't have any except our private riding stock."

"Alice is a good rider, too. Do you have sisters?"

Ben told them of his family, and Mrs. Farris said that she would like to meet his parents and sisters.

"My mother is a bit like you, Mrs. Farris. My sisters

will like Alice. But don't expect too much of my step-father, Wesley Bradford. He is—well, you will have to draw your own conclusions about him."

Jack jumped up. "I think mother is trying to tell us that dinner is ready."

Ben noted that Mrs. Farris did bring out her best china. He was almost afraid to touch it. She had turned the tailgate of the wagon into a table. Before eating they all bowed their heads—which was strange to Ben—and asked the Lord's blessing on the food. As they ate, they asked about the country and the people living there. Between mouthfuls Ben tried to tell them. He remembered what his father had said in derision about Mormons, but these people were nice. All they wanted was a home. If they were what Mormons were supposed to be, Ben liked them.

Dinner over, they sang a hymn and had another prayer. After a few minutes rest, Jack Farris stood, picked up the ax, and said kindly, "You will have to excuse us, young man, there is much to do. Come along, Phillip."

"I will help," Ben volunteered.

"Very well . . . we can use all the help we can get."

The man and two boys set to work with a determination to get something done. Ben proved his strength in helping handle the logs. He was no stranger to an ax. Phillip was not far behind but wanted to stop and talk to his new friend, which drew a kindly rebuke from his father. Of course they had to hurry. The cabin had to be finished soon. Some of the clear land had been plowed and planted, but more remained to be cultivated. They had already missed the spring rains that were so

19

necessary for a good crop.

Toward nightfall Ben felt that he must leave—his mother would worry if he were late. While he had the run of the countryside, he still felt a responsibility to her. The work was taken care of primarily by Fred. Their crops were all in and Fred kept them plowed for the most part—such as should be plowed. But the horses were Ben's responsibility. Wes liked the way Ben understood them. Sometimes he even had his son accompany him on horse-buying trips, but not often. Wes did not like his family to be alone at night on the farm, so Ben usually stayed home. During the days of inactivity the forest was his second home. Sometimes when Wes was not away Ben would make camp along some woodland stream and stay a while, surviving by his skill as a hunter.

Chapter 3

The next few days were happy ones for Ben. While his stepfather was away on a buying trip, Ben had hitched up the carriage and taken his mother and sisters over to meet their new neighbors. The women had gotten along very well and Becky and Flo immediately became friends with Alice. He also noticed that Phillip took some sidelong glances at Becky. There had been a picnic—Caroline had prepared a basket of delicious food to add to the plain fare of the Farris household. The men continued to get the logs ready to put in place. Help came one day in the form of a group of people that Ben had not met, and the work went unusually fast. They were a part of the Saints who had migrated west with the Farris family. Ben found them to be a happy people, although they spoke with a different accent and seemed to be more educated than the Missourians. The cabin went up in a hurry when they came. They started the day with prayer, which was interesting to Ben. A big rawboned man named Johnson seemed to be the leader. With his powerful body, moving those logs in place was a simple thing. He would laugh as the others grunted with their loads. He seemed never to tire. The women and girls put chinking between the logs. Within two days the cabin was complete except for a board floor. The ground would have to do for a while. Ben liked the way these Saints shared the work, and he had much to tell his mother and sisters about them.

After the cabin was finished Ben noticed that the Farris larder was practically bare, so he proposed a hunt the next day with Phillip. The father gave his approval. Long before daylight Ben was at the Farris cabin. Phillip had slept in the wagon so he would not awaken the rest of the family at that early hour. The boys slipped quietly way from the cabin and mounted Comanche, where Ben had left him with the guns. In a short while they came to a stream where deer often drank. Ben gave Phillip specific instructions about what to do.

"Now stay close to this tree. When a deer goes to the water to drink, take your rest against the tree. Get him the first shot, because you won't get another. Don't even snap a twig. He'll hear it and be gone."

Ben moved over to another tree nearby. He wanted Phillip to get the first one. It was beginning to break day when he heard something coming down the trail. It was a nice fat buck. Phillip saw it. . .aimed. . .shot. . .and the deer fell. Ben always felt a sadness for what he had to do, but the deer had to be bled. After this was done, he brought up Comanche. The horse did not like the load the boys put on his back and pranced about a bit, but Ben calmed him down. They tied their kill onto the saddle and headed for home. While on the way, Ben stopped. He had heard a familiar sound—a turkey. Tying the horse to a bush, the boys quietly moved near an open space among the trees. Ben took something from his pocket, stuck it up to his mouth, and made the sound of a turkey. He was answered. He did it again and again until a gobbler came into the clearing. This time Ben did the shooting.

The boys rejoiced as they approached the cabin. The Farrises were up and about. Jack and Virginia hugged both the boys while Alice voiced her pleasure. "Which one of you got the deer?" she asked.

Phillip strutted a little and replied, "I did. Ben let me have the first shot. And one was all I needed, eh, Ben?"

Ben agreed. "He's a good shot. He didn't need me to help him. I hope he can have a gun soon. He'll need it for game. There is lots of it around."

The two women took the turkey and plucked it while the men hung the buck on a tree limb and skinned and dressed it. It was fresh at this point and needed to be aired out, so they formed a tripod of tree limbs and hung the meat up where other wild animals would not get it. Coyotes and wolves were numerous in the area.

"I'm going to buy Phillip a gun just as soon as we are able," Jack said. "I was always more interested in books than firearms. Teaching is my profession. By the way, Ben, when we get our seed planted and are waiting for it to mature I want to start classes for my children and any others nearby who wish to attend. If you and your sisters want to come I'd like to have you."

"That would be great," Ben answered. "None of us have had much schooling, but mother has taught us to read. I've learned to cipher a little too."

"Then if your parents agree, we'll start as soon as possible."

The turkey was dressed and immediately put to roasting. Ben and Phillip had had no breakfast, so Alice fixed some leftovers and served them under a shade tree. Jack had taken the ax and gone out to where he was clearing land. After eating, Ben and Phillip stretched the deer skin and prepared it for curing; then Ben left for home because he was expecting Wes back with more horses. He felt better, knowing that the Farrises would

23

not go hungry. He supposed that they had some money to get along on, but the venison and turkey would help.

Wes had come back and, with George's help, was driving the horses into the pasture when Ben arrived. For a change Wes was in a jovial mood. The Indian went home. It had been a long trip, and he was tired. Wes went into the house, and Ben heard his sister squeal with delight. He knew that was Flo. Becky was growing up now and showed her pleasure of Wes's return a little more reservedly. They all came out to see what Wes had bought.

There was a chestnut mare with one white stocking that caught Ben's eye. "I believe you have something in that mare," he told Wes.

"Work them over good, and we shall see."

Ben and the Indian spent several days with the horses, so he did not see his new friends for a while. The mare with the white stocking was fast; so one day he rode her over to the Farris' cabin. Phillip gave the horse an admiring look, and Ben let him ride her. Then Alice wanted to try it and Ben helped her on and let her ride for a while. The whole family had been busy clearing land for crops. The womenfolk had helped by gathering up the brushy limbs and burning them. They had shared the venison with their friends, and it was about gone, so another hunt was planned. Jack wanted to go this time.

Ben enjoyed the ride home. White Stocking, as he called her, rode smooth. He let her run hard just before he reached home. She was also a racer. Wes would be proud. He unsaddled and walked her around the lot until she cooled down. Wes was in town; and at this point Ben had said very little about the horses.

On the day of the hunt, Ben was at the Farris cabin long before daylight. The three hunters walked into the forest to Ben's favorite spot, and Jack did the honors this time. The deer was not as big as Phillip's had been, but it would do. They tied its legs to a pole and carried it back to the cabin. After skinning it, they cut thin strips to dry in the sun. Then Ben spent some time helping Phillip make traps for smaller animals to be used for food. It was too early for furs. They would build traps for that when winter came.

Ben had said very little to Wes about the new neighbors and his association with them. He did not want him to know how deep the relationship was becoming. He did speak of the Farrises, however, and said they were nice people. He also mentioned that they had a boy his age, and asked if it would be all right to share one of the horses with him. Wes, knowing that the horses needed to be ridden, said, "Have the boy help you exercise the animals."

Phillip had little spare time, but Mr. Farris thought it was good for him to help with the horses. So nearly every day Ben would take an extra one for Phillip, and they would go for a gallop over the countryside. Ben soon discovered that Alice wanted to be a part of this venture, and that pleased him, so he began taking over two. Usually he let her ride Comanche. Even though he had two sisters to whom he talked quite freely, their conversations had been limited. This was different somehow. He liked the way she moved about the cabin when he was there, and her quick smile when he was near.

Ben and Phillip were sitting on the top rail of the

corral at the Bradford home one day watching the horses mill around when Wes rode up from a trip to Independence. Ben could see that he had been drinking and cautioned Phillip.

"Well, have you got those horses ready to sell?" Wes asked in a surly voice.

"Yes sir," Ben replied. "You made a good buy on this bunch. Two of them could make you some money as racers—especially the chestnut with the white stocking. The other is not far behind."

"This the boy you were telling me about?"

"Yes sir. This is Phillip Farris, Papa. He's a good rider."

Before Phillip could acknowledge the introduction Wes commanded: "Saddle up those two horses and let me see what they can do."

Ben said, "Yes sir," and he and Phillip jumped down from the fence. They took a rope from the post and, singling out the horses they wanted, saddled each in turn. Ben wanted Phillip on White Stocking to impress Wes, so he chose the other.

"All right, I want you boys to ride down and circle that lone oak tree at the end of the lane and back when I give the signal." Wes raised his pistol and fired. Slashing the horses with the end of their reins and kicking them in the flanks, the boys bent low in the saddle, each trying to outrun the other. They rounded the tree together but White Stocking took the lead coming back and won by half a body length.

"I want you to give these horses special care," Wes said. "I've got a buyer coming tomorrow, but put these in a stall; they are not for sale just yet. Don't curry them yet, I don't want anyone to know that they are important. If we don't say much about them, I can make more money in a race. After that we'll spruce them up like gold pieces. Then I can sell them for more money. Give them some grain. . . they're worth it."

Ben and Phillip did as they were told. After they cleaned up, supper was called, and Phillip was invited to stay. A Negro woman did the serving, which was strange for Phillip, but he said nothing. The conversation was of an idle nature until Wes spoke up.

"I keep hearing in town that the Mormons are about to take over our county."

Ben looked at Phillip and noted the color in his face. He also knew that Wes was purposely baiting his friend.

"Not to take over the county, sir," Phillip said straightforwardly. "Just to find a place to live."

"Then I take it by your remark, young man, that you are one of them."

"I am, sir."

"Why?"

"Sir, I believe in God. I believe that he directs people who will listen to him as he did long ago. I believe that he directed our people to this wonderful land."

"To drive us out? To take over our land and free our Negroes?"

"Oh, no sir! We don't want your land or any of your property. It is true, however, that we do not believe in slavery. We want only the privileges due all Americans—to worship our God and to live in this beautiful place."

"I'm afraid you Mormons have bit off more than you can chew." With that he turned again to his food.

27

Ben felt deeply for his friend, and later as they rode the buckskin back to the Farris farm, he felt he had to talk about it. That was the beginning of an evening Ben would long remember. He knew of the Whitmer Settlement to the southwest, and west of that, the Big Blue Settlement. Still further on was Colesville. All these Saints had settled in the last several months. He had taken grain to be ground at their mill and they had treated him well. Mormons! The word was usually said in such a way that it sounded ominous. He could not imagine Phillip being dangerous to the community . . . and most certainly not Alice. He was determined to hear more about these people.

Chapter 4

"Mormons are not bad people," Phillip said as they jogged along. The late summer sun was filling their eyes with its brightness. "We came here because we feel that God directed our prophet to do so."

"Now you've got me... talking about a prophet."

"We believe that God has a prophet today the same as he did in Bible times," Phillip explained. "Why shouldn't he—after all, God is unchangeable."

"All right, suppose there is a prophet. Does he go around in a long white robe and tell us we are doomed as the ones in Bible times did?"

"The times that I have seen him, he was dressed in broadcloth or work clothes like my father or yours. He is tall and well built. He played ball with us the last time we were together. When the men get together during a picnic, someone usually challenges him to wrestle, and so far nobody has pinned his shoulders to the ground."

"Why do so many people resent you Mormons?" Ben asked. "Before I met you I heard lots of bad things. Of course, folks repeat stories whether they are true or not. Where did the word Mormon come from anyway?"

"We'll soon be home, and my father can tell you better than I can. That is, if you would like to listen."

Ben said he would.

When the boys arrived they found the Farrises sitting in the shade of a large elm tree. They arose to welcome Ben as usual. Mrs. Farris gave him a hug; Jack gave a warm handshake. Alice smiled and said, "Hello." Jack and Phillip had made some chairs, spending precious money for lumber to do so. Phillip went into the cabin and brought two more out for Ben and himself. Ben's thoughts were on Alice as all this was going on. The way she brushed her hair back in a nervous little gesture when she was talking to him. She could bake bread, ride a horse, work in the garden, or make a dress. He felt that his sisters could learn a lot from Alice, and he felt a shy joy when he was near her.

"Ben and I have been talking about the prophet," said Phillip to his father. "Wes brought up the subject of all of us moving in here and how people are afraid we will take over. I explained some things, but I left most of it for you."

"That's right, sir. Please tell me what it is all about."

"It started with a young man in New York State. He was younger than you," Jack Farris began. "As a matter of fact, he was fourteen years old. He had been attending some revival services in the neighborhood and was deeply concerned about them. One day he opened his Bible and read in James—the first chapter, fifth verse—'If any of you lack wisdom, let him ask of God, that giveth unto all men liberally and upbraideth not; and it shall be given him.' This struck deep in his heart. Although he was still just a boy, he felt he had to know, so he went to a wooded area near his home, knelt, and asked God for knowledge. He had a vision. . . just as men of old used to have. He saw two personages in a shaft of light. One pointed to the other and said, 'This is my beloved Son, hear him.' When he asked what church to join, he was told to join none of them. . . that God had a work for him to do. That was in 1820. Three years later he had another vision as he retired to bed. He had been unkind to his parents and this bothered him.

Thinking of his sins and desperately wanting forgiveness he asked God for a sign if he had been forgiven. Suddenly the room was full of light. An angel stood in that light and started to talk to him. After quoting various passages of scripture, the heavenly visitor told him—among other things—that hidden in a hill nearby was a record of the ancient inhabitants of this land. It was a record of their contact with God, of how they had come to the Americas, built their civilization, and then became wicked. They are known now as the American Indians.

"The next day this young man, Joseph Smith, went to the hill he had been shown in the vision and found the spot where the record had been placed. A round rock was sticking above the ground. Prying it up, he saw a stone box. This contained plates of gold. The angel reappeared, forbidding him at that time to take the plates which had records written on them. He needed to mature first; however, he was to return to this place each year until he was ready for the work God had for him to do. This he did. In the meantime, he met and married a fine young woman. On the fourth visit to the hill he was given the plates with the admonition to protect them with his life. I might add that it did almost cost him his life. He was faithful, and through the power of God he translated the records on those plates, then returned them to the angel. This translation is called the Book of Mormon. It complements the Holy Bible, reassuring all who read it that God really did 'so love the world.' Joseph Smith is a wonderful person and a true prophet.''

"I would like to meet him," said Ben. As Jack had

been speaking he had experienced an inner warmth—a kind of glow he had never felt before.

"More than likely you will, since he has designated this area as the gathering place. To us, this is the New Jerusalem."

"What do you mean?" Ben asked.

"We believe that one day we are to live in an area where we can be at peace with the world and every neighbor will be a friend."

"Then why are so many people afraid of you?"

"Not all Saints have been careful in what they have said. Because we call this our 'inheritance,' some people think we are going to take the land away from them. But we are to buy our inheritance, not take it from others. Many believe we will cause an uprising among the slaves. While we do not condone slavery, we are still admonished to leave the property of others alone—that includes their slaves. God will take care of the matter in his own time. Another thing that bothers some people is that we believe God still speaks. I think that because we say an angel visited Joseph Smith, they think that we are a little crazy...or that we think we are better than others."

Ben felt the sincerity of the man. After all, he was educated far beyond the average person. This religion must have appealed to his intelligence as well as to his spirit.

Jack interrupted his thinking. "Let me say this: The Book of Mormon in no way destroys the Bible. It is a history of several groups of people who migrated over the sea and built up civilizations in this part of the world. They were both righteous and unrighteous...

good and bad at different times. They, too, had their prophets. Sometimes they listened to them, sometimes they killed them. Sometimes they did great things; sometimes they did terrible things. They were most righteous after Jesus' visit following his resurrection. He confirmed that 'God so loved the world that he gave his only begotten Son.' After the ministry of Jesus these people went into a golden age. Everything was going well. . .then they started to dictate to God how they would worship. They became proud. They fought among themselves. American Indians have a wonderful heritage."

Phillip went into the cabin and returned carrying a book in his hands. "Here, Ben, is the book. Examine it. . .it won't hurt you."

Ben took it. As he turned the pages he found the statement of three witnesses. These men had been shown the plates by the angel. They knew that Joseph Smith had translated them by the power of God. So intense was Ben in his examination of the book that he did not notice the Farrises were all staring at him.

"If you like we will get you a copy to read. . .or we can read it together as we have time," suggested Jack.

Tears were in Virginia's eyes. "You see, Ben, we have learned to love you. We do not want to lead you astray or cause friction in your family. We will get you a copy of this book if you wish, but we are not going to push it on you."

"Mother will say very little about it. Wes is a different matter. I don't believe it will cause trouble as long as I keep my work up with the horses and help Fred when he needs a hand. I'm glad you explained this to me. I want a book, but I think I would like to join you folks in reading it. At least you can get me started on it."

Jack spoke again. "You see, Ben, people can call us what they want, but this church was organized in 1830 by six young men by the command of God through his Son, Jesus Christ. It *is* the Church of Jesus Christ. Because we have a testimony of this, we have to take our stand, whatever the cost might be."

Chapter 5

Summer moved into autumn. Wes Bradford sold most of the horses he had purchased except the two fast ones. Sometimes Ben and Phillip would take them on a long run together. Wes usually referred to Phillip as that "Mormon" kid, but he liked the way he handled horses. He was disappointed when Phillip refused to ride in a race for stakes, saying his father would not approve of the gambling involved. Wes left it at that, but Ben rode White Stocking and won a good deal of money. Wes was so pleased that he shared it with Ben. Then he said that if the Mormon kid had ridden the other horse, he would have won more money, even at second place. White Stocking was a winner. Ben kept her curried until her coat was beautiful and shiny. Wes told Ben she was so good that they better race her while she was still not well known or they would not be getting any bets.

Ben and his sisters started to school with Jack Farris as teacher. On warm days classes were held outdoors under the elm tree. Ben became familiar with more words, and as time passed he found that reading the scriptures became easier. After the students mastered the few readers available to them, Jack used the scriptures for teaching.

The majority of people in the community had not yet seen the importance of a school. Most of them could not read or write, and lived in windowless cabins. Ben's folks were from the South and had received some education, especially in the rudiments necessary to conduct their affairs in an intelligent manner. Caroline had been brought up to enjoy the finer things of life, and she had taught the children to be polite and courteous. She had insisted that they study during the winter months under her tutelage, and they were not far behind the Farris children. Sometimes she had Ben hitch up the carriage, and would go visit with Virginia while classes were being held. Ben was pleased that the two women got along so well. Wes chose to ignore "that Mormon family."

Ben and Phillip were fortunate in most of their hunts to bring in enough meat for both families. Deer, small game, and turkeys were plentiful. The boys set snares and a few steel traps to catch fur-bearing animals, thus making some extra money during the winter. Eventually Phillip had saved enough to buy his own gun. Ben took an extra horse for him, and the two of them rode into Independence to the gun shop and made a selection. They could hardly wait to get out of town to try it. It proved, as the gunsmith had said, to be in good working order.

Ben had read the Book of Mormon and found it interesting. He could not get his mother to read it, but she did read the testimony of the three witnesses in the front of the book. Her only comment was, "I like the Farrises...they are very nice...but don't get too mixed up with their religion."

On April 6 Ben hitched up the carriage, drove over to the Farris place and picked up the family. There was to be a celebration at the Big Blue Settlement that day—it was the third birthday of the church, which was organized in 1830. Everyone was in a festive mood. There was hymn singing and a prayer meeting. When this was over, food was spread out on improvised tables. From

36

the looks of the tables, Ben couldn't tell that it had been a hard winter for these people. He noted that they were happy. There were games for the children and wrestling for the young men; in this he proved his ability, pinning his opponent's shoulders to the ground twice. He received a warm handshake all around, even from the young man he wrestled.

After the games, Ben moved closer to Alice. She looked up and smiled. When he took her hand, she did not pull away. They left the troupe and strolled down by the river.

"Doesn't spring smell wonderful?" Alice took a deep breath. "This is the best time of the whole year."

"It means lots of work when it is not raining—plowing and planting." He hesitated. "You know, Alice, I like you. . . I like you a lot." Then his tongue seemed to become tied and he could not talk.

Alice took hold of his arm, squeezed it, and just smiled. After a while she said, "That was nice, Ben. I want you to like me. I know we are too young now, but we won't always be. Right now we will just like each other and let that be enough."

"With your Papa's permission we could go riding together. And I guess he won't mind if we sit in church together."

"I don't think he will mind. They tease me about you."

"Do they? My sisters tease me about you, too."

"You know I think Phillip is sweet on Becky. I tease him about her and he gets all red-faced."

"Wouldn't that be something! I'd like it. . . Becky and my best friend. If we can get him to ask her, I can bring her along when we go to church, and he can sit with her. I'll put in a good word for him."

"I really don't think you need to. Haven't you noticed how your sister looks at him? I have."

"I've seen him giving her sidelong glances, but she acts like he isn't there."

"You just watch the next time they are around each other."

They laughed over their secret. The object of their conversation sauntered up at that moment and, hearing their laughter, wanted to know what the joke was.

"We will tell you sometime but not now," his sister said.

"The party is getting serious now. The men are getting together to talk about our problem. I guess I should be there," Phillip said. "They don't want to spoil the fun everyone is having, so they are talking quietly in the shade of that big maple tree."

Ben glanced over toward the tree and saw the men gathered there. "I think you should, too."

"It's getting bad. Another brother was dragged out of his bed last night and beaten in front of his family with his kids screaming 'Don't hit my Papa.'"

"Won't the local sheriff do anything?" Ben asked.

"He's probably one of them. We wrote to the governor but he just gave us a play of words. No one pays attention to him. He doesn't seem able to enforce the law. Two of the men rode to Lexington to see the judge and that did no good either." Phillip turned on his heel and walked toward the men, leaving Ben and Alice alone with their thoughts.

In late afternoon the Saints dispersed. Cows had to be

milked and other chores done. Ben stood by as Jack helped his wife into the rear seat of the carriage and climbed in beside her. When Ben helped Alice into the seat beside him, Phillip looked puzzled for a moment; on the way to the celebration *he* had ridden beside Ben.

Jack suggested, "Why don't you young folks sit in front? Mother and I will just tag along back here."

Alice moved over closer to Ben to make room for Phillip. Ben liked that, but felt his face redden. As they headed for home Virginia started a song, and soon they were all singing. Phillip got off key and they all laughed at him. Perhaps that is why they did not notice the danger until suddenly the carriage was surrounded by armed riders. The horse stopped as one of the men grabbed the bridle. Ben knew him. His name was Chambers. The man turned his head slightly, keeping his eyes on Ben, and spurted a stream of tobacco juice. He wiped the spittle off his chin with the base of his hand and said, "You don't care who you associate with, do you, Benny boy?"

Anger flooded Ben's whole body. "Get your hands off that bridle, Chambers, and get out of my way."

The man laughed. "I bet old Wes is sure proud of you, boy, takin' up with these d____ Mormons."

"These are my friends. Now get out of the way!" He wished he had his gun.

"So I see. Well we are going to chase your friends clean out of the country," Chambers threatened. The other men yelled out in agreement. They all had rifles cradled in their arms.

Ben felt Alice trembling beside him. He looked closely at the faces of each man. He wanted to remember who

39

they were. Jack's quiet voice from the rear seat relaxed the tension somewhat.

"We mean no one any harm, sir. May we pass, please? You are frightening my wife and daughter."

Chambers doffed his hat and bowed. "We never want to frighten the lovely ladies." He moved, and Ben whipped the horse. Harsh laughter followed them as they rode away.

Chapter 6

April blended into May, and the Saints plowed their fields and planted their crops. Ben was helping Fred, and had less time to spend with his friends. Even the enemies of the Saints had work to do and therefore campaigned against them less during this period. The incident following the April 6 celebration had not had any repercussions. Ben had said nothing to his mother because he did not want her to worry; he also had cautioned the others to say nothing. Once while in town he had met Chambers, who had grinned and given him a knowing wink as he passed. Ben felt anger boiling up inside him. He would like to hit the man with all the power he possessed. Even if he could get in only one good blow, he thought, it would be worth it.

Sunday was the best day of the week for Ben. He would hitch a horse to the carriage, pick up Alice and her family, and go to church. Sometimes his mother and sisters went along. When they did he would turn the carriage over to the parents after reaching the Farris home, and the young people would walk the two miles to church. The services impressed Ben, but he had a hard time understanding how a man could get in front of a group of people and talk for two hours. Sometimes he saw some of the Saints nod. Once he heard a snore and Alice, sitting next to him, giggled. Her father turned from his seat in front and frowned. Later as they rode home in the carriage her father chided her about her behavior, then he started laughing.

"Jack Farris," Virginia said, "why reprimand your daughter when you thought it was funny too?"

"Well, I could see the man. His head was tilted back, and a fly kept flying around and landing on his nose. In his sleep he kept swatting at it. Then he gave that big snore."

"If you saw all that you were not listening to the sermon. I guess I will have to punch you in the ribs with my elbow every once in a while to be sure you are paying attention," his wife said.

"If you are fretting with me you won't get anything out of the sermon," he laughingly answered her.

Ben, Alice, and Phillip in the front seat smiled at this dialogue. Anyway, Ben thought, the Farrises had a good sense of humor.

Becky still held Phillip at a distance. When she went to church with the family she would let him sit with her but she would ignore him when he was that close. Ben noticed that she did look at him at other times when she thought no one was watching. Girls! It was like Wes once said, "You'll never understand them."

It had been planned on one such Sunday in late June for the Farris family to have Sunday dinner at the Bradford home. That morning Caroline and the girls planned to go with Ben who had arranged seats in the wagon so all could ride and come back to the Bradford farm. Wes had gone to town saying that he wanted nothing to do with the activities. Caroline seemed to be relieved that he would not be there, although it was a discourtesy. She and Blanche and the girls had prepared on Saturday for the meal. It was a beautiful day. The woods were fresh and green. The corn was up and would soon be "laid by," which meant it would need no more plowing. Except for hoeing the gardens, there would be a little more time now for other things. Ben was fortunate in that Fred could pretty well take care of the farm. Of course the haying would have to be done, but cattle and horses ran on most of the Bradford land.

Fred harnessed up a good team to the wagon and they set out in high spirits. Caroline was laughing as the Farris family climbed in that morning. Alice took her place by Ben, smiling in a way that had come to mean so much to him. Phillip smiled at Becky, and she smiled back this morning, pulling her skirts closer so that he could sit beside her.

Services were held under the big maple tree. The speaker was interesting, and Ben could see that his mother was taking it all in. The man who had snored at the previous service was not asleep this time, although as the memory passed through Ben's mind he could not resist smiling.

The ride home was pleasant. Virginia told Caroline of Jack's correcting his daughter and how he himself had become tickled in the process.

"The man did not go to sleep today," Jack added. "We had an exceptional speaker."

"You certainly did," Caroline said. "Perhaps you can explain some of the things he said a little more thoroughly to me after we eat."

"I will be glad to."

Flo had been silent the whole trip, and Ben wondered if something was wrong with her. He would have to see when he got a chance. He noticed that she went straight to her room when they arrived home. Blanche had the food about ready to put on the table when they came in the door. Ben excused himself and went to find Flo. She was in her room, sitting on the bed and staring out the window.

"What's the matter, little sister?" he asked as he seated himself on the edge of the bed and put his arm around her.

She burst out crying.

"Come on...tell your big brother," he said soothingly.

"Everyone has someone except me. You have Alice, and Becky has Phillip. I'm just a tag-a-long."

"You are more than that. You are my sister, and I care for you. It's just that I'm eighteen and almost a man. Becky and Alice are young women now. Phillip is as old as I am. Two or three more years and you will be the age we are now. You are very pretty...and you will be even prettier, I'm sure."

"Do you really think so, Ben?" She put her arms about him.

"You bet I do."

When dinner was announced, Flo dried her eyes and went with Ben into the dining room. Ben smiled and pulled back the chair for Alice. His mother presided over the dinner in true southern fashion. She was always the gracious hostess. Ben thought that perhaps the absence of Wes was a good thing. That opinion was verified before the dinner was over and Wes entered.

"Well, well, well...look at the Mormons at my table!" he exclaimed.

Silence filled the room. Blanche, coming in from the kitchen, stopped. Ben heard Alice catch her breath. Jack half arose from his seat. His mother gained her composure first.

"Wesley Bradford," she commanded, "either leave the room or sit down before you fall down."

Ben had never heard his mother talk like that to Wes. Seemingly Wes had not either. He sat down.

"Blanche, fix him a plate and a place at the table."

"Yes, ma'am."

Jack stood and said, "We do not wish to cause you any embarrassment, Mrs. Bradford. I will take my family home." Virginia started to rise.

"Both of you, please sit down. . .you are my guests. In the morning Wes will be ashamed of what he has said, although you needn't expect him to apologize."

They sat back down, and Blanche served Wes although she frowned while doing so. Scowling, Wes ate some of what was before him and left the room. Soon he was snoring in the adjoining room, and Ben remarked that it sounded a bit like the man at church. This brought chuckles and relieved the tension. The boys took chairs out on the shady porch for the women and Jack, while Blanche and the girls cleared the table. Ben and Phillip checked the horses until the girls came to the porch also. Then they joined the group. Evidently Caroline had asked Jack a question concerning the morning sermon, and Jack was still answering her:

"These two young men, Oliver Cowdery and Joseph Smith, went down by the river and, finding a quiet place, knelt in prayer. They had not considered baptism until they learned about it while working on the translation of the Book of Mormon. They wanted to know what they were to do about it. While they were praying a heavenly messenger came to them and said that he was John the Baptist. He laid his hands on their heads and ordained them to the priesthood of Aaron. This gave them a certain amount of authority, but they were told that when the Melchisedec priesthood was given to them later it would carry much more authority. Then they went into the water and baptized each other, as the angel had told them to do. Immediately after baptism the gift of prophecy was given them and they foretold of the rise of the church in the latter days. It was to be restored as it existed in the days of the apostles. This had been prophesied by the ancient prophets, and now it was coming to pass. With the Lord's continued blessings they organized his church on April 6, 1830.

"The Melchisedec priesthood was restored at that time, and elders were ordained. These men had authority to lay hands on the converts and pray for them to receive the Holy Spirit. We use the laying on of hands for various ordinances. One is the blessing of babies; we do not baptize infants; instead we bless them as Jesus did. Remember, he said, 'Of such is the kingdom.' We who are older are to be baptized to have our sins washed away. Another ordinance is the blessing of the sick; we anoint them with oil, lay our hands on their heads, and ask that God through his Son Jesus Christ will heal them. This is in keeping with James, the fifth chapter and fourteenth verse: 'Is there any sick among you? Let him call for the elders of the church; and let them pray over him, anointing him with oil in the name of the Lord: and the prayer of faith shall save the sick, and the Lord shall raise him up; and if he has committed sins, they will be forgiven him.' We take this seriously. You see, God *had* organized his church through his Son Jesus Christ and has authorized it to build his kingdom here on earth."

Virginia was moved by Jack's explanation. "I think I understand a little better, now. As you say, the Book of Mormon tells of God's love for all people, even the early inhabitants of this land. It does not replace the Bible, but is another witness of Jesus Christ. I see now why Ben is so interested. . . aside from your lovely daughter, of course." And she laughed at her son's embarrassment.

Chapter 7

July came, and trouble began to break out again. Most of the local citizens had resented the Saints for some time. Then an editorial appeared in the church publication, *The Evening and Morning Star*, establishing their neutrality on the issue of slavery. This infuriated the Missourians of southern sympathy. There *was* no neutral ground on the slave question as far as they were concerned. If the Mormons were not for them, they were against them. From various parts of Jackson County a mob gathered in Independence on the day a horse race had been planned. It was into this situation that Ben and Wes rode. They had heard of the rioters long before they reached town and wondered what was going on.

When they arrived it was easy to see that no one was interested in the horse race. Groups of angry men were walking the streets of Independence firing guns in the air and visiting a keg of whiskey someone had conveniently set up for them. Ben recognized several men who were shouting about what they were going to do to the Mormons. Prominent among them was Chambers, who gave Ben a leering grin. Ben gave him a hard look in return.

"Let's tear down their printing press," one of the drunks yelled.

The cry was taken up by others, and axes began to appear. Ben saw the mob carry out the printing press and scatter the type in the street. Men with axes were busy with the structure. The Phelps home was invaded, and Mrs. Phelps with a sick child in her arms was

48

pushed into the street. She was crying. Some of the mobbers ran into the store of Gilbert and Whitney, grabbed bolts of cloth, and ran down the street unwinding the material behind them. As dusk began to settle they captured Bishop Edward Partridge and Charles Allen.

"Where is the tar bucket?" someone yelled, and a man came running with a bucket. The struggling captives were held tightly while several of the men tore their clothes off and poured tar on them. A pillow was brought from the Phelps home, cut open, and the feathers poured onto the tarred men.

"Now let's cowhide Partridge," someone yelled.

That vote was lost as someone started making sounds like a partridge calling for his mate. The mob started hopping about, making the partridge call, their drunken laughter ringing out.

Ben looked at Wes. He thinks this is great fun, he thought, and wondered if Wes would join the mob. His stepfather only stood and watched, as did a number of other citizens. Nobody offered to help the victims. As far as that went, Ben didn't know what to do either. Yet, what if these were his friends who were being pushed around. The thought of harm coming to Alice filled him with anger.

A yell went up, "Let's get 'em all while we're at it. Get your horses, men."

Another yelled, "Let's have a drink first."

For the first time since their arrival Wes spoke, "I don't give a d____ about the Farris family, Ben, but if they were *my* friends I'd get on the fastest horse and ride to warn them." With that he walked away.

As Ben headed for the horses Chambers stepped out to block his way. Ben did not know whether he had heard Wes or not. All Ben knew was that Chambers was in his way. Without saying a word he gave the man a quick jab in his face and buried his right fist in his midsection. Puffs of dust came up around the larger man as he sat down hard on the dirt road. Ben spent no time waiting for the man to get his breath. In a fleeting glance, however, he noted a bleeding lip.

White Stocking stretched her legs in a mile-eating run. It was not far to the Bradford farm where he stopped long enough to tell his mother of the situation. "Bring the Farrises if you can—we will hide them," she said as Ben quickly mounted and headed for the Farris home. He hoped the mobbers would spend lots of time at the whiskey keg.

The clatter of the hoofs as he approached the cabin in the clearing brought Phillip and Jack to the door. Ben called out to them, and his warning brought instant action.

"Mother, you and the children go with Ben to their place. I will do what I can, then hide nearby and see what happens," Jack said hurriedly.

Phillip started to remonstrate, but his father would have none of it. "I fear that they have already killed some of our people, and I don't want to lose one of you."

In the gathering darkness Ben helped the women mount White Stocking and head for the Bradford place. He and Phillip walked.

Jack, thinking of Virginia's pride in her fine china, hurriedly put it in the box that had carried it from New York and ran with it up the hillside where he hid it in some brush. Then he hurried back to the cabin to retrieve Phillip's gun and some ammunition. He knew that one gun against the mob would be of little use, but he didn't want it falling into enemy hands. He drove the pigs and the oxen deep into the woods, where they could fend for themselves. That was all he had time to do before he heard the sound of horses. Hiding on the hillside in some brush, he watched the yelling mob break out the two windows that had cost him so much to install. Then one man climbed up on the roof and tied a rope to the chimney, and a horseman toppled it over. The same man tied a rope to part of the roof while another tied the other end to the saddle horn and pulled the roof off. Although it was night, the moon was up, and Jack could see almost as if it were day. He sighted the rifle on the man on the roof but did not pull the trigger. No sense in adding fuel to the fire—even to protect his home. Finally the mobbers, laughing and yelling, headed for the settlement on Big Blue. Jack followed on foot running and walking in turn. He heard gunfire before he had gone very far and speeded up until he heard the horsemen returning. Hiding alongside the road, he watched them go by, then went to the ferry and halloed across. When he was recognized, someone came over to get him.

The enthusiasm of the mob had waned by the time they had reached the settlement. They mostly shot into homes and raced up and down the street scaring the people. One man received a superficial wound.

Seeing that there was nothing for him to do, Jack wearily turned his attention to his family. On the way to the Bradford farm he passed his own place and tears came to his eyes. He and Virginia had had so much hope. Ben rode up as he was meditating and told him that the family was safe. . .praise God! He mounted Buckskin, and rode behind Ben to the Bradford home.

With the arrival of morning Blanche put breakfast on the table. Wes remained in the bedroom. Caroline wisely suggested that they eat before going over the happenings of the night before.

Breakfast over, they sat around the table and talked. Jack told his experience first, then Virginia told theirs.

"After we left you and were going down the road we heard riders coming. Ben took us into the woods, and we made it safely to the Bradfords. Ben scouted the barn and house, then got his mother's attention. She let us in, and we all sat here in the dark praying for you. In an hour or so we heard the mobbers returning, and Ben and Caroline put us in the root cellar. We heard the riders stop and call for Wes. Wes wasn't here, but he did come up the lane soon after they arrived. We heard a lot of loud talk and learned that they were disappointed they had not found you. That relieved us. Even though they laughed about what they did to our cabin, we were grateful you were not caught. Pretty soon Mr. Bradford came down into the root cellar and got a jug. I guess he saw our faces when he opened the cellar door, but he never said a word to us. One of the men called out, 'Wes, you need help findin' that jug?' Wes answered, 'You stay there, Jake, I'm coming.' After they all had a drink, I heard Wes say, 'Don't you think you've had enough excitement for one night?'

"'I reckon we have. Let's go home, men,' someone said, and they rode off."

At that point in the story, Wes entered the room. Jack stood up and offered him his hand and started to thank him. He ignored the hand and sat down at the table. Jack thanked him anyway, but Wes did not answer. Ben looked at Jack and made a helpless gesture. Blanche brought coffee, and Flo, who had been silent, went up to her father and put her arms about his neck and kissed him on the cheek. Wes brightened and put his arm about her. The girls could do more to soften him than anyone. His whole attitude seemed to change and, without looking at Ben, he said, "Ben, I think a certain Mr. Chambers don't like you very well. I turned around, saw what you did to him, and went over to help. He had a time getting his breath back. . . and one front tooth he won't get back!" Wes began laughing.

Then Ben told him of the incident on the road and of Chambers stopping the carriage. Wes studied that over. Ben continued, "That's not why I hit him. I thought he might have heard you say what you did about saving my friends, and planned to stop me. I couldn't let him do that."

Phillip said, "He had it coming."

"Now, Phillip. . . don't talk like that," his father chided.

Wes looked at Mr. Farris directly for the first time. "Turn the other cheek business I suppose."

After the conversation slowed down, the Farrises said they had better leave. Ben hitched up the wagon and put some tools in it. After arriving at the cabin they set to work. Two men from the settlement showed up, and before the day was over the Farris home was again habitable.

Chapter 8

Ben heard from a neighbor who stopped in to look at some horses that more trouble was brewing. The men of the area were organizing a militia to drive the Saints out of the county.

"We're going to get rid of 'em or kill 'em," Sam Plummer exclaimed. "What do you think, boy?"

"Mr. Plummer, sir, I think it would be better if you let them be. Have they ever harmed you?"

"No, and I ain't goin' to let 'em."

"Well, why don't you wait until they bother you? They have never been a problem to anyone; in fact, they've been helpful. Flo, Becky, and I have been taking some schooling from them."

Plummer gave him a hard look. "Does your pa know how you feel about this? If he finds out, he'll skin you alive. These people are *bad*. They're goin' to make our slaves restless. Why they even claim that God Almighty talks to them. I never heard the like! If we don't stop 'em now they'll rule the state, and you know what *that* would mean."

"I *don't* know what that would mean . . . nor do you."

"If it wasn't for your pa and me bein' friends and all, I'd give you a thrashing, boy."

"That is your privilege, sir. And I would count it a pleasure for you to try."

"Well, I was in the market for a horse, but now I'm out of the notion."

"These horses are gentle broke, and I don't want to sell one to you anyway because you don't appreciate good horseflesh. Good day to you, Mr. Plummer."

54

His face red and contorted with anger, Mr. Plummer mounted his horse and rode away.

I'll catch it when Wes finds out, Ben thought. He did. Wes swore at him and threatened to strap him. He was driving his customers away all because of those d___ Mormons.

"I forbid you to see any of them again," Wes stormed. "All they have done is cause trouble."

"That's not true, and you know it. My sisters and I have received a little more schooling because of them. Phillip helped with the horses. He and I are good friends. His family has been good to us."

"Nevertheless when a man comes to buy a horse I don't want you insulting him. Sell him a horse if he will pay our price."

"I will just tell you the way it is, Papa. They better not insult my friends. Remember it was you that suggested I warn them when we thought the mob would harm them. Another thing, I may become one of them." Ben startled himself with the statement. Wes gave him a hard look and walked away. Ben had not really ever thought of himself as a Saint...just a friend who understood and liked the people. For the next several days he was ignored by Wes. Wes sometimes kept himself isolated from others in the family even though they might be in the same room with him. Occasionally Flo and Becky would put their arms about him and—if his mood was right—he would swing them around until they squealed with delight or became dizzy and fell to the floor.

While in a happy mood one day he let the girls each pick a horse and invited the whole family to take a long

55

ride. After packing lunches they saddled up—Wes on his favorite mount, Caroline on Kitten, and Ben on Comanche. They took the Mormon ferry across Big Blue and headed west; they planned to cross the state line and visit a village of Indians in Kansas. As they went by McKeever's store, a hangout for anti-Mormons, they saw some horses at the hitchrack, but no one appeared at the door. The Colesville Mormon settlement was a few miles beyond, and as they rode into the village, some of the people recognized Ben and waved. They were stopped before going on through by big Joel Thompson who insisted that they come in and visit. Wes tried to refuse, but Becky and Flo saw some girls their age in the doorway and begged to stop. Mrs. Thompson was very pleased. She pulled out the only two chairs they had for Wes and Caroline. The girls went up into the loft bedroom to show some treasure they had to Becky and Flo. Ben sat with Joel on the rough sawn bench, while Sarah Thompson busied herself at the fireplace where she was baking pies. She talked to Caroline as if she had known her for years. Wes sat quietly observing the woman's dexterity. When Joel praised the Bradfords for helping the Farris family, Wes remained noncommittal. Ben could hear the girls giggling up in the loft. It was a pleasant, peaceful moment enhanced by the aroma from the baking. Soon Sarah set two hot pies on the table and said, "Now you must have some. There are more for the rest of the family, and I insist that you have some of these." She reached in the cupboard and brought out plates and forks.

Ben and Wes had just taken their first bites when there was a clatter of horses' hoofs . . . then the firing of a gun. The girls came down the ladder. "It's the mob again," one of them cried, cringing in fear.

"Now everyone be calm," Joel said. "Maybe it's just a ride through."

They all went to look out the window, but Joel pushed the girls back. A rock came crashing through the window, and the flying glass cut a gash in Joel's face. Everyone else ducked. They heard a scream.

"Oh no, they are dragging old Brother Sutton out. That was his wife screaming. She will die of a heart attack if something happens to him." Joel went to the door.

"Don't go out there," his wife cried. "They'll kill you."

"They will kill that old man and she'll die right along with him. I *must* go," he said and went out to face the mob.

The girls were whimpering. Ben could see that Sarah had bowed her head and was praying silently. Standing at the broken window Ben and Wes could hear all that was said. Joel was trying to get to the elderly man who was on the ground, moaning and asking them to leave him alone. Two of the mobbers were pummeling him and obviously enjoying his discomfort. Joel grabbed one of the men and threw him into the air. Then he grabbed another and jerked him away. Just as he was reaching for another a man hit him over the head with a pistol, and Joel went down. Two of the mobbers grabbed the big man, dragged him to a hitching post, and tied him to it. Another tore his shirt. Sarah screamed, and ran out the door. One mobber shoved her away, and she fell to the ground. The blacksnake whip wielded by a burly fellow curled around the upper part of Joel's bare body. Ben bolted out the door, grabbed a stick of wood, and without thinking of his own safety waded into the mob. The men tried to stay clear of this angry avenger who was yelling as loud as they were. Suddenly he realized that he was not alone. Wes was beside him and he, too, had a stick of wood. The mobbers began to retreat even though they far outnumbered their attackers.

"Wes...Wes...what are you doing to us?" one of them shouted. Wes now had his hand on his pistol as old Mrs. Sutton ran to her husband and Sarah went to untie Joel. He had come to and was standing dizzily as she worked to free him.

"What's the matter with you, Wes?" the man with the whip demanded. "These are just Mormons."

"They may be Mormons but we were partaking of their hospitality, Gates, when you men showed up. Now that was not polite. These people could teach you a lot about manners. Now you know I don't like to be interrupted...especially when I'm enjoying myself. You interrupted me and I'm mad, and my son, Ben, here, is mad. If you don't leave I'm going to turn him loose on you, and you already know what he can do. Or Mr. Thompson. The three of us will make a team." He put his arm around Ben...something he hadn't done for years. "Tell 'em, Ben," he said.

"Gates, I know you...and all the rest of you. Now, get out of here," He raised his club.

Wes spoke, "You heard my son, Ben. He can outshoot and outfight and outride the lot of you. I think you better take his advice."

After the men had left, Wes finished his pie, giving it

58

the praise it deserved. He had enjoyed his part in the fracas. He even spoke sympathetically with the Thompsons about their predicament. "It's not over. They'll get drunk and come back another time. What are you people doing then?"

"We've tried the governor, but he just refers our case back to the local authorities who are in with the mob. What *can* we do?"

Sarah was dampening cloths and placing them on Joel's wound. Wes shook his head, gathered up his family, and went home—the trip to Kansas forgotten.

Ben and Wes became real friends that day. When word of what had happened got out Ben was ostracized by some of the neighbors. Wes told and retold in the saloons how his son waded in on the mob like a wild Indian. The account was blown out of proportion, but a lot of people enjoyed that kind of story. Nevertheless more trouble was brewing for the Saints. One night a group of drunken rowdies rode to a lone cabin, dragged the man from his bed, and flogged him in front of his wife and children. Ben—always armed—made more frequent trips to see his friends.

Chapter 9

South of Big Blue community was another village called the Whitmer Settlement. On the night of October 31, 1833, fifty-one armed men attacked the sleeping settlers. Little children were screaming in mothers' arms as their fathers were dragged through the streets and beaten with clubs and gunstocks. Some were tied, stripped, and horsewhipped. A few escaped into the woods where they were hunted like animals.

Awakened by the boisterous mobbers as they returned from the attack, Ben arose to find his parents looking out the window. One of the men called out, "Ben Nelson, we just took care of a bunch of your Mormons. Come on out and we'll take care of you next."

At that moment Wes stepped out on the porch. Pistol in hand, he leaned against a pillar and shouted, "Now you listen to me. I know who you are, and if you harm anyone in my family I'll kill all of you. Remember, I'm no Mormon so I can shoot back."

Ben ran to his room, pulled on his riding clothes, and returned to where his folks were standing. "I'm afraid something has happened to my friends." He took his rifle off the pegs on the wall. "I've got to see about them."

Wes said, "You go, Ben. I know these men. I'm going to town and get a few things straightened out before this goes too far. Here is one of my pistols. In a running fight, it might be handier. I know how the Mormons feel about firearms but somebody has to protect them."

"If the Farrises want to come back here, they are welcome," Caroline said.

Wes agreed.

Caroline was worried. "I want you both to be careful. I can't afford to lose either one of you. Wes, you know how headstrong you are."

"Ben's the one to warn," Wes told her and laughed. "I'll never forget what he did with a stick of firewood. And that Thompson fellow was willing to sacrifice his own life for that old man! This thing just can't keep going on."

The girls came out of their room rubbing their eyes as Ben ran out of the house, leaving his mother to explain. What if the mob had attacked his home, he thought. His sisters would be frightened. No doubt he would be dead, for he would fight to the finish. He knew that the presence of Wes at the Thompson home was what had made the mob back off. He could not have lasted long without Wes's help, but he would have tried.

Comanche needed no urging as Ben headed for the Farris cabin. Reaching his destination he slid to a halt. The cabin was badly damaged. When Ben halloed his presence through the darkness, Alice answered.

"In here. . . we're in here."

He dismounted and ran into the cabin. Moonlight was coming in through the top of the house—the roof was gone. Alice ran into his arms crying. Jack was lying on the bed, and Virginia was sitting beside him. Phillip lit a candle, and Ben saw so much blood he thought Jack was dead. A moan reassured him that the man was still alive.

"I think the mobbers have gone to town for liquor. You shouldn't have to worry about them returning tonight," Ben said.

The figure on the bed twitched in pain. "Ben, you watch Phillip for me. He wants to go after them with a gun, and I don't want that...God doesn't want that."

"I'm not so sure that I don't want to help him," Ben answered. "Do you feel as if you can ride, Mr. Farris? Mama says to bring all of you over to our home...and Papa agreed."

"He hurts so bad, I think he hates to move," Virginia looked up at Ben through tear-swollen eyes. "They beat him terribly."

There was the sound of horses' hoofs and wagon wheels coming toward the cabin. Phillip snuffed out the candle. Ben stepped outside and flattened himself against the wall with the pistol in his hand. It was Fred. Caroline had told him to hitch up the wagon and follow Ben to the Farris home.

Fred and the boys carried Jack—tick mattress and all—and put him in the wagon bed. Virginia and Alice climbed in beside him. Phillip jumped up behind Ben on Comanche. Fred drove as carefully as he could, but Jack still groaned when they hit a bump.

Phillip told him the story. The mob had ridden into the yard and shot all their pigs. He grabbed his rifle, but his father told him to shove it under the bed...one shot from it would get them all killed. Some men climbed up on the roof and tore it off again. Alice and his mother were cringing in a corner. When his father went out to try to reason with the mobbers they knocked him to the ground. Phillip had tried to help him, but two men grabbed him and held him while his father was stripped and whipped. Virginia ran to him but they held her and made her watch as they cut Jack's back to ribbons.

Then they went into the cabin and broke all the china. "Now get out of the county," they shouted and rode away.

"They didn't harm my sister. . . just looked her over and laughed at her fear, but they left her alone, thank God." Ben felt his blood boil.

When they arrived at the Bradford home Fred drove the team up to the porch steps, and Caroline ran out to help. Flo held the door open while the men carried Jack in and put him on a bed; he had passed out during the ride. Blanche set fresh corn bread and butter on the table for anyone who might be hungry. When she saw Jack's back she threw up her hands and cried, "This old woman know what to do; she fix a lot of hurts."

She mixed up an herb mixture which she and Virginia gently rubbed on Jack's wounds. As they worked with him, Jack roused and asked for Ben and Phillip.

"I wish you boys would ride over to the Whitmer Settlement and see what has happened to the people there. I am deeply worried about them. . . . Tell them I am praying for them."

Before Ben and Phillip went out to saddle up a horse for Phillip, Wes came in. There was a bruise on his left jaw and a bit of swagger in his walk. When he learned that Jack was hurt, he went in and spoke to him.

"I'm afraid we will cause you trouble, Mr. Bradford," Jack said.

"Call me Wes. . . and don't worry about it. Some folks like me and some don't. I don't much care one way or another, but I feel I owe you an apology, I have been rude to you in the past even after what you have done for my children—giving them that schooling, I mean.

Now don't get me wrong, I'm not getting religion. I just think enough is enough for a group of people to go through. You and your family are welcome here as long as you have need. I've learned a lesson in all this. That fellow Thompson taught me something, and then Ben's action finished it. You have the protection of my home and of me while you are here."

His speech finished, Wes returned to the dining room and sat down at the table. Blanche brought him a cup of coffee, which he lifted with both hands. Up to that point no one had noticed his hands. Seeing them, Caroline asked with alarm, "What happened to you, Wes?"

He looked at his swollen hands for a moment and started to laugh. "I should have had your stick of wood, Ben. Fistfighting is hard on hands." Then he said, seriously, "Nobody is going to ride up to my door and threaten anyone in my household and get away with it. I just had to go to town and prove it."

"You might have been killed!" Caroline exclaimed.

"That's right, I might have. . . but my statement still stands."

Ben went up to Wes, put his arm around his shoulders, and gave him a squeeze. Neither one said anything but the message was clear.

A few minutes later the boys mounted and headed for the Whitmer Settlement. To reach it they had to take the ferry across the Big Blue. The Saints there were greatly disturbed. The mob had held the ferry for a while and threatened them but had done no actual damage. Some of the men had gone to the Whitmer Settlement but had not returned. The boys turned and rode south a short distance to the little community. It was devastated.

Roofs were torn off cabins; chimneys were on the ground; windows were broken.

Some men were gathered around a fire in the middle of the village. Among them was a Mr. Johnson, with whom Ben was acquainted. The few houses that were still intact were being occupied by women, children, and the men who had been beaten or otherwise hurt.

Mr. Johnson greeted the boys and explained what had happened the evening before. When Phillip told him about his father, the man shook his head. "It has come to the point that we will have to take up arms and defend ourselves, or be killed or driven from the county. The people in Clay County, across the Missouri River, had offered us a refuge. I just don't know what to do. These are our homes. We bought the land and built them. Why should we leave?"

"Do you have food?" Phillip asked.

"A little," was the reply.

"If you have a team and wagon, send someone to our place. They killed all our pigs last night," Phillip said. "I'm sure that my father would agree in this."

Two of the men volunteered and left immediately. Mr. Johnson turned to Ben and smiled. "We have heard how you fought for our people at the Colesville Settlement. That papa of yours must be quite a man, too."

Phillip spoke up. "You should have seen him after the mob stopped at their place and threatened Ben. While Ben was coming for us his papa went to town. When he came home he had a bruise on his jaw and two swollen fists. He just laughed about it, but it was easy to know what had happened."

"We are told to seek redress for wrongs from the officials of the county, but how can we get help from them when they are afraid of the mob? Some, in fact, are in the mob. We are having a meeting at the Big Blue Settlement later this morning, Phillip, if you want to come. Ben, we appreciate all that you have done and are doing now, but we don't want to get you into any more trouble than you already are. We are going to discuss taking up arms for our protection," Mr. Johnson told the boys as they were mounting to leave.

"I'll be there. Papa is not able, of course." Phillip answered.

Later, as they passed the Farris place they saw the two men loading the pigs. Back at the Bradford home they found Blanche frying sausage and eggs. The boys cleaned them up as quickly as she put them on the table. The two families were asleep except for the girls. They were talking softly as Ben and Phillip went by their door. Ben knocked softly, and Flo let them in. Alice came over close to Ben and he took her hand. His sisters started to giggle until he frowned at them. Phillip moved close to Becky, but she backed away. He shrugged his shoulders as if it did not matter. Becky's face grew solemn at that gesture, but she said nothing.

After telling the girls what they had seen on their trip to the settlement, the boys went to Ben's room and lay down for a brief rest before the meeting.

Chapter 10

The meeting at Big Blue Settlement was half over by the time the boys arrived. The argument to take up arms was a heated one. After three days of meetings, the men decided to defend themselves. Ben was not there when they reached that decision. His mother had become worried when she saw so many armed riders going by in groups at various times during the day, and looking toward the house. Wes laughed at her fears, but Ben had stayed home while Phillip had continued going to the meetings.

Ben had loaned Comanche to Phillip, but he had not returned—which was unusual. Ben had waited up for a while, then had fallen asleep in front of the fireplace. Awakening suddenly he saw lights flashing on the wall across from the window. He jumped up and looked out—the barn was on fire. Yelling at Wes he headed for the door. The whole west side of the barn was in flames. Wes ran out behind him, stopping only long enough to pull on his boots.

"White Stocking is in there," he cried. Ben was already running for the barn door. Jerking it open he ran in. White Stocking was rearing and stomping.

"Ho, girl, ho!" Ben released her from the stall, leaped on her back, and made a dash for the door. His mother opened the gate to the pasture and he rode through. Then she closed the gate, because she knew that horses have a tendency to return to their stalls even in a fire. While Wes and Fred carried riding gear out of the lean-to saddle shed attached to the barn, Ben ran to the water tank and grabbed a bucket.

Wes saw him. "Won't do any good, Ben . . . it's gone."

By this time some of their neighbors came riding in with buckets in their hands. They had not even taken time to saddle; a fire was everyone's business. Fred produced a ladder, and water was carried up and thrown on the roof of the house. Fortunately there was little wind, and few sparks went in that direction. All anyone could do was to watch and put out other fires that started. Luckily the winter hay was stacked in the meadow away from the barn. A smaller stack at the side of the barn had been the source of the fire. There was no doubt in anyone's mind that it had been set.

A bearded neighbor named Riggs sidled up to Wes and asked, "You suppose this is the work of them fellers you had a fight with?"

"I better not find out for sure," Wes said.

"Everyone knows you are harboring Mormons in your house," Riggs spoke again. "They don't like that a-tall."

"They can not like it and be d_____ as far as I am concerned. A man ought to have the right to feed his family and live out his life any way he chooses as long as it does not interfere with his neighbors. You know that, Riggs."

"I know, but these Mormons are dangerous. We don't want them taking over our land and tryin' to free our slaves."

"They bought that land fair and square. I didn't want them here at first, but then I found out that they are better than us in manners and concern for each other. We could use a little more of that in this community. Have they ever hurt you in any way?"

"Well, no, but. . ."

Wes snorted. "Thanks for coming over, Riggs, but there's not much to do now—the barn is about gone. I'm glad there is no wind to carry sparks to the house or haystack."

Blanche called out that she had cider poured for everyone.

Phillip still had not appeared, and Ben approached Wes with this information.

"Give him another hour, then come and wake me if I'm asleep. Don't tell the others of your worry," said Wes.

But the others were already worried. They had noticed that the boy was missing. Jack Farris could get around pretty well now, but his back was still stiff and uncomfortable. Virginia got Ben and Wes aside where her husband could not hear, and spoke of her concern.

Wes said, "He is a smart boy, Mrs. Farris—I think he can take care of himself. We must keep Jack from worrying. If Phillip doesn't show up soon, Ben and I will go look for him."

Wes did not go to bed as he had planned. Instead, after all the neighbors had gone, he and Ben stepped outside for a conference.

"Saddle the horses while I get into the rest of my clothes. I'll have Blanche fix us something to eat, and we'll go looking for the boy."

Ben said that he did not want to eat, but Wes told him that he would need it—a soldier could not travel far on an empty stomach. While they were eating, Comanche came home. They found him standing by the corral gate when they left the house.

Wes ran his hand over the saddle and checked the riderless horse. "There is no blood. Maybe he just fell off somewhere."

"Not Phillip—he's a better rider than that. I know that he was going to the Big Blue Settlement to a meeting. He took his rifle with him—I helped him slip it out so his father would not see."

Ben unsaddled the horse that he had previously saddled, now that he had Comanche to ride. All that remained of the barn as they passed it was a bed of red embers. They left as quietly as possible and headed west. Wes had a brace of revolvers in his belt and his rifle in the saddle boot. Ben also had a rifle. Comanche knew his every whim and would respond to either word or body signal. He had shot game from his back and the animal did not flinch. He was not as fleet-footed as the mount Wes rode, but he could be ridden for long distances without tiring. Ben felt that he might need Comanche's stamina and power before the day was over.

As the two men rode they could see the horses' breath in the frost air.

"Let's go see your friends on Big Blue first—they might know something," Wes said.

"All right."

Wes had been exceptionally quiet up to that point. Ben knew that the burning of the barn weighed heavily on the man, but right now finding Phillip was more important. When they reached the river the ferryman came immediately for them.

"Have you seen Phillip?" Ben asked. He knew the man well.

"He was here yesterday. We had some trouble, and he went with the men to help settle it." He eyed Wes speculatively and hesitated to say more. Ben saw his hesitation.

"This is my father, Wes Bradford... Mr. Coates." The introduction was acknowledged by both men.

"Oh, you're the one." Memory flooded the ferryman's face. "I've heard about you." He grasped Wes's hand and pumped it vigorously. Wes gave him an amused smile. Mr. Coates went on with his recitation of events. "You probably heard yesterday how a bunch of ruffians the night before attacked a house where a man lay sick. He had insisted that his wife and children run and hide leaving him there. The mob broke in and beat him with gunstocks. They said they were going to kill him and fired a shot which creased his head. Then they tore off the roof of his cabin. Someone took a shot at the men and wounded one of them. Our man is in bad shape but will live. So will theirs. They came and took the ferry away from me, but they didn't destroy it. I guess they figured they would need it. After scaring us all half to death they rode on."

"You were lucky—they burned our barn and we're not Mormons," Wes said. "Go on... we're trying to find out what happened to Phillip."

"I'm coming to that. Phillip rode in here yesterday morning on that horse, and went with a few others to Colesville. When they heard the sound of firing, they grabbed their guns to go help. There was a battle. Two on each side were killed. Word is out that the militia is being called to arrest the Saints. Phillip may have been picked up by some of them. He wasn't with our people

71

when they regrouped. Of course men went out to look. Maybe he has shown up at the Whitmer Settlement or made it back to Colesville. Come to think of it, your horse showed no sign of being in the river, did it? Now if the mob is pulling some shenanigan, they would have had to cross at the ferry north of here at the mouth of the Blue. That brings in the picture that they wanted you to get the buckskin."

Wes turned to Ben. "What do you think, son?"

"Papa, it's a trap. This horse came in right after the fire. I believe they wanted us to find them. You are the one who turned on them in front of their friends in town. Now they could have killed either one of us during the fire, but that would not have been fun to them."

"You may be right, Ben. If they could have killed White Stocking they would have gotten some revenge on us for the races we have won. They know how I love that horse. Let's ride and see some more of your friends."

The men in the Whitmer Settlement knew nothing of Phillip. Some of them were living in makeshift shelters. The sadness in the faces of the women got to Ben, and he could see that it touched Wes, also.

They gave McKeever's store a wide berth until they could talk with someone in Colesville. It was well into the morning when they reached that village. Ben thought of all that had transpired in the last several months. These good people had been beaten and their homes destroyed—why? Because they were of a different religion than the earlier settlers? Or was it because they believed that God speaks, that angels visit the earth? Many of the townsmen could not understand that people could believe this and still be good. Maybe the major problem was that they claimed to be neutral on the slave question. Most Missourians said that you were either for or against slavery—there was no neutral ground. They were afraid the Saints' stand on slavery would cause trouble among their slaves.

Ben's thoughts were interrupted by the sight of big Joel Thompson standing in front of his house. The family came out, welcomed them, and insisted they eat breakfast. As they ate mush and milk, Ben asked how the Thompsons had managed to keep their cow. Joel had to admit he did not know. Wes turned on the charm and soon had the children smiling in spite of their problems.

Unfortunately Joel did not know what had become of Phillip, so Wes and Ben said they had better be on their way. Joel asked if he could pray for them before they had left. He put his powerful arms around both of them, and prayed a prayer unlike any Ben had ever heard. He patted each on the back and gripped their hands in turn.

"I hope the good things you people have done for us will not cause any more problems for you. Whatever our fate, I'm glad our paths have crossed. I'm willing to go with you to look for Phillip if you need me."

"No," Wes said. "I've got a hunch where he is. I feel sure they want us to find him. They've probably set a trap for us. You have enough troubles—we'll handle this one."

As they mounted Wes said, "McKeever's store."

Ben said, "Right."

Chapter 11

"Ben, how's your nerve?" Wes asked.

"First rate," came the answer. "What's on your mind?"

Wes pulled up and stopped the horses. He hooked one knee over the saddle horn and contemplated the landscape.

"There are a couple things we can do now. Since your friends don't know what happened to Phillip, he must be in the hands of the enemy. One thing we could do is to lay out near the road to McKeever's store, their meeting place, capture someone who comes along, and see what he knows. The other plan is to ride right up to the store as if we owned it, walk in, and face the situation. I'm sure that the burning of the barn and the disappearance of Phillip are related. They burned the barn, then turned the buckskin loose to come home. I've got a feeling that they were nearby, hiding out while the barn burned."

Ben agreed.

Wes went on. "To have killed us, at least then, would have spoiled their fun. That would have ended the matter. They enjoy prolonging the torment. Now, if they have Phillip they'll use him to draw us to them. They haven't forgotten what happened at the Thompsons that day when it looked as if I changed sides—which I did in a way. I surprised myself really, Ben. When I saw you sail into those men without a thought for yourself, I figured if my son is brave enough to do that for these people then I ought to side up with him. I thought those men would take it as a good brawl, and later in town we could drink together and forget it. But it didn't turn out that way. All right, that's enough talk for today, let's circle McKeever's store. If we can capture one of the men, maybe we can get him to tell us a thing or two."

They rode part of the way, then hid their horses and cautiously approached the store from the northeast. Keeping to the woods, they circled to the front. There were men going in and out the door. Horses were at the hitchrack. Ben was all for crawling up to a back window and looking in, but Wes would have none of that. It was not long before a couple of men came out, mounted their horses, and headed toward Wes and Ben's hiding place.

"Let's see who they are," Wes said. "We're too near the store to make a capture—the ruckus would be heard."

The men came close, riding at an easy gait. Ben knew them. "Let's go," Wes grunted. Carefully they ran to their horses, mounted, and Ben took the lead. He knew the lay of the land better than Wes. When they had passed where they supposed the men on the road would be, they cut back to their right and secreted themselves behind a thicket. They didn't have long to wait. The men approached, laughing and talking, unaware of any danger. Wes pulled one of his pistols, and Ben checked his rifle. Looping the reins over the saddle horn, Ben nodded to Wes and they rode forward blocking the way of the approaching riders. The men's mouths dropped open at the sight of the guns pointed at them. One of them started to reach for his pistol only to be stopped by Wes.

"I wouldn't if I were you," he said. The man put his

hand back on the saddle horn.

"Let's get rid of those guns," Ben commanded.

The men complied, eyeing them speculatively.

"Now, let's all get down," Wes added. "Keep your hands in sight while you dismount," he cautioned. "We don't want to shoot, but don't think for a moment we won't."

One of the men was a burly fellow. Ben knew him as Sloane. The other—a slim man—was Jackson.

"All right, men, sit down," Wes commanded.

"Here on the cold ground?" Sloane complained.

"Here on the cold ground. You don't seem to mind making the Mormons sleep on the cold ground, so sit!"

"We want to know two things," Ben said when Wes was through. "First, what became of Phillip Farris; and second, who fired our barn last night."

"We don't know anything about that," Sloane answered. "All we know is that there was a fight, and a couple of our boys came up missing. I suppose they are dead or the Mormons have them."

"Who is at the store?" Wes asked.

Jackson spoke up. "Wes, you got no call to treat us like this. You ain't a Mormon. Why you takin' up fer them? They're just a bunch of idjuts bustin' in our country tryin' to stir up trouble."

"They are people. I was all for it when the so-called fun started, but it didn't take me long to mend my ways. Now, I want to know who is in that store. Do they have a prisoner?"

Wes cocked his gun, his face reddening with anger. Speaking through gritted teeth, he said, "I haven't got all day, Jackson. Are there any prisoners in the store?"

The thin man's eyes wavered as he looked at Sloane, but Sloane was noncommittal. He swallowed. "One," he said. "A boy about your boy's age."

"Who burned my barn?" Wes went on.

"I don't know anythin' about that except I heard some bragging. They was so much drinkin' goin' on after the fight I cain't remember. Sloane knows more about that than I do." Sloane kicked Jackson and glowered at him.

Wes shifted the gun to Sloane, and Sloane spit at him. Wes spoke to Ben. "Keep your eye on Jackson. I'm going to give Sloane a part down the middle of his head—just like they gave that sick fellow the other night. Just keep in mind, Sloane, I'm not a Mormon, and I don't turn the other cheek."

With that remark, Wes squinted down the sights of the pistol. Sloane wavered. "All right. . .all right. . . hold it!"

"Give me the *whole* story," Wes commanded.

"Well, it was like this. After the fight we had, this kid on the buckskin," he nodded toward Comanche, "he was a fightin' fool. When he didn't have time to reload, he swung his rifle, and he bumped several of the men real good. Then someone knocked him off his horse. Willis caught the horse, loaded the boy on, and took him to the store. He's in the back room. Gates got the idea that since you and him had a row to hoe over that fight you had, we'd take the buckskin back close to your place. Seein' that the boy was missin' you would go on the warpath. Him and the others, the ones that you and this boy here tangled with, got the idea to burn your barn and get that racehorse of yours at the same time.

They was all likkered up. I guess if they had not had so much to drink, your barn would still be there. Anyways, that's what happened. They watched the barn burn, then turned the buckskin loose so it would go home with a empty saddle and worry you some more. They figgered that you would come lookin' for 'em and they'd get even."

"The barn wasn't enough?" Wes asked.

"I reckon not."

"These men are at the store waiting for us, right?"

"Right."

"How many?"

"Six."

"Three for you, Ben, and three for me—that ought to make it about even. The boy is in the back room. Is he hurt bad? Tied up? What?"

"Well, he walked in the store. I guess he ain't hurt too bad. I think they tied him up. . .I didn't really see."

"What are we going to do with these two?" Ben asked.

Wes had a twinkle in his eye. "Do you want to shoot them?"

"Oh no!"

"We've got to do something with them. We can't have them giving out an alarm to their friends. Of course they won't have any friends when they find out that these boys told on them. Of course they want us to find them and walk into their trap. If we ride up to that store ignorant like, they might shoot us. If we set the place on fire, the Mormons would get the blame—and they have enough troubles without that. If they weren't drinking so much they would have guards posted. Do they have guards posted?"

Jackson looked at Sloane, and Sloane dropped his eyes. "Yes and no. They have some, but they got into the whiskey keg so often they're hardly what you'd call guards." He added, "Gates and Willis are cold sober."

"All right. You gentlemen have been very cooperative. We'll let you go," Wes said.

They got up off the ground and started to mount.

Wes spoke again. "Not that way—you walk. Take your boots off."

Jackson started to complain, "The ground's too cold. We need our boots. We'll catch our death."

Wes said, "I know. I saw some little Mormon children barefoot today and without shelter. I saw some grown men and women without proper clothing for the cold. They shared their mush and milk with us. You have destroyed their crops and homes. When your feet get cold, think about all the damage you've done to these people. That will warm your heart and your feet—now get!"

The two men pulled off their boots, exchanged glances, and began limping down the road.

Chapter 12

When they were out of sight Wes turned to Ben, "All right, son, we better hold a council of war. Do you have any ideas? The most important thing is to get Phillip out of there. Now we'd better get rid of these extra horses. We also have two extra pistols for our use that these gentlemen so kindly contributed."

"We could wait until dark," Ben said, "but that's a good four hours away. I don't think I can stand it that long. We could get some help from our friends in the neighborhood, but they've had enough trouble already. It would bring on a shooting battle and someone would get killed."

"Yeah," Wes said thoughtfully. "Let's handle it ourselves. "I'm the one they're really after. If I ride up to the front door real bold and divert their attention, you could sneak up to the back, get in the window, and free Phillip."

"Yes, but they might shoot you. They know how dangerous you are. I could more likely get away with it."

Wes studied that over for a moment. "All right . . . maybe you can pull it off. Here, stick one of these pistols in your boot top. It's a little uncomfortable but not as uncomfortable as being unarmed in an enemy camp. Don't pull it if you don't have to."

Ben stuck one of the confiscated pistols in his boot top and pulled his trouser leg over it. The bulge showed, but as Wes had said, it was better to have a little insurance. They tied the captured horses to a tree. Someone would eventually see them and untie them.

Wes rode around to approach the store from the rear.

Ben knew that his stepfather would have to get situated where he would have an open space behind the store to cross. A lot depended on how much the men had been drinking. He knew, of course, that he would have to deal with the sober Willis and Gates. He mounted Comanche and loped up to the store. A man who was lolling outside saw him and ran into the building. This was Ben's chance. He dismounted at the hitchrack where six other horses were tied.

Leaving his rifle in the boot on the horse, he opened the door and walked in. Seven men, including McKeever, looked him over. Ben ignored the six and turned to McKeever.

"How do, sir," he said in greeting. He unbuttoned his coat. That movement caused one man who was leaning against the wall in a chair to drop the chair legs and become more alert. Ben ignored him and went on. "I've lost a friend . . . a Phillip Farris. Have you seen him, sir?"

Ben looked around as if for an answer. They were all there—Jenkins, Willis, Gates, and the burly fellow who had wielded the whip at Thompson's place. He didn't know the other two.

"What kind of horse was he ridin'?" one asked.

"My buckskin out there at the hitchrack."

One man made a thing about going to the window and looking out. "Well, well, boy, that's a fine horse you got there." He grinned as if having a private joke. "What makes you think that we might know where your friend is?"

"Well," Ben spoke slowly, "he was heading for the settlement when I loaned him my horse. He's a

Mormon, and I heard there was a squabble of some sort. I know you men don't like Mormons, but he is my friend and I kind of look after him."

"You bring a stick of wood with you this time?" the burly fellow asked and laughed. "You and your pa thought you had us scared at the settlement the other day."

"Yeah, I did kind of get carried away. I should have known better. If Papa hadn't been carrying a gun, you men would have mopped up the ground with me."

Gates spoke up. "We ought to know. Why didn't your pa come with you? Is he afeared or something?"

"The barn burned down, and he was going to get some men to rebuild it. Have you seen my friend?"

"What sort of lookin' feller was he?" asked one of the men Ben did not know.

He described Phillip.

"Ain't seed him a-tall," was the answer. "Why did you say your pa didn't come?"

"I said. . ." and the men began to laugh.

Ben acted embarrassed, but he kept his eyes on Willis and Gates. Like the captives had said, they were cold sober and dangerous. Looking at him speculatively, Gates said something to Willis who pushed past Ben and went out the door. Oh, good Lord, I hope he doesn't run into Wes out there, Ben thought.

"You don't suppose," asked Jenkins, "that your pappy was too scared to come and help you look for your friend?"

The implication was too broad. Ben had to take exception to it.

"What do you mean, 'too scared'?" He had to act

insulted or these men would not believe him; his whole act would fall apart. He started for the man bristling for a fight. This was better than he had planned. It would give Wes more time. He should be at the back window by now—probably figuring out how to open it without creating a disturbance.

McKeever spoke up for the first time. "You fellers want to fight, go outside. Don't tear up my store."

"Well, I'm ready," Ben said, feigning anger. The men were excited. A fight would make their day. They all made a move for the front door. Gates looked around, apparently for Willis and, not seeing him, went with the men.

Ben shucked his coat and threw it over the saddle of Comanche. Jenkins had his coat off and they squared away. As they circled around, Jenkins made a rush with arms outstretched to grab Ben. Ben sidestepped, shot out his foot, and Jenkins stumbled. As Jenkins was going down Ben hit him on the jaw. Someone grabbed him from behind until Jenkins got up swinging. Ben kicked the shins of the man holding him and dropped to the ground as the man loosened his hold. Jenkins' blow missed. Ben knew that that one would have hurt, for Jenkins was the bigger man. He was going to have to end this quick. He did not have any idea what had happened to Wes but hoped he was moving while the excitement lasted. Bracing himself, he shouldered a blow aimed at his jaw. He felt it throughout his body, even though it did not land where Jenkins had aimed. Ben sidestepped another blow and got a good lick with his right in Jenkins' face. Before the man could shake the cobwebs out of his head, Ben delivered a hard one to his midsection. Jenkins had been drinking, and the blow made him sick. He fell to the ground vomiting. It was at this point that Ben heard Wes laugh.

Every eye was turned toward the sound. There was Wes with a pistol in each hand. Phillip was standing beside him. Ben thought that he'd never seen a more wonderful sight.

"Let's get those hands up high, gentlemen," he commanded. Quickly they obeyed.

Ben pulled his gun from his boot, although he didn't need to. Wes had them all covered. He stuck it in his belt where he could easily reach it if necessary and started collecting the guns from the men.

"My, son, that was a fine piece of work you just did. I couldn't have done better myself." Wes was in his element. "Now, you and Phillip take all the guns including the rifles in the store."

Mr. McKeever opened the door, started to come out, changed his mind, and slammed the door. He opened it again when Wes warned him that he was going to shoot up the place if he didn't. Ben picked up the rifles, brought them out, and laid them at the feet of Wes along with the pistols.

"Did you meet Willis behind the store?" Ben asked.

Wes laughed. "I met him . . . he's sleeping now. He made the mistake of sticking his head in the window after I had opened it and climbed in to free Phillip."

About that time Willis came around the building shaking his head to clear it. Seeing the commotion he started to run. Ben caught him and brought him back.

"Ben, you and Phillip take the guns and throw them in the well," Wes commanded.

There was a cry of protest.

Wes laughed. "What did they cost you? Twenty, thirty dollars apiece? What about my barn? I have it on good authority that you burned my barn. Do you think you could redeem them by rebuilding my barn? Mr. McKeever, come out here."

McKeever came to the door.

"Bring paper and pen and something to lay the paper on. I want you to do some writing," Wes commanded. When Mr. McKeever had nervously brought paper and pen and a box to lay it on, he sat on the edge of the porch and looked up at Wes.

"How shall we word this?" Wes asked. "Put this down: We, the undersigned promise to rebuild for Wes Bradford and his son, Ben Nelson, one barn which through our fault was destroyed. We will furnish lumber, nails, and labor. In exchange for this they will return our guns, which will be held by Mr. McKeever until the job is completed." When the paper was finished, Wes read it and passed it on to Ben. Another copy was made, and the men marched up grudgingly to sign both copies.

While Ben was unloading the guns, Wes was talking.

"Well, gentlemen, this has been a profitable day. We now have in our fold one lost Mormon boy. We will expect you on the following week to start building our barn. Gates, you seem to be the leader—see to it that it is done. I have a paper signed and witnessed by a leading citizen of our county who believes with all his heart in law and order. Isn't that right, Mr. McKeever? By the way, you are an officer in the state militia. They could not find a better, braver man. Let me make it quite clear, gentlemen, that no one of my household or the friends of my family will be mistreated over this incident. We want to thank you for taking such good care of our friend Phillip."

Ben went with Phillip and McKeever to find a place to lock up the guns. As McKeever started to pocket the key, Ben shook his head, took it, and put it in his own pocket.

Going out the door Ben and Phillip heard Wes giving the men a sermon on their morals. The "congregation" took it in sullen silence.

"Let's look at it this way, men," he was saying, "I could take your lives; instead I'm giving them back to you. All right, boys, turn these gentlemen's horses loose so they won't have any temptation. I'm tasting some of Blanche's good cooking right now."

Ben and Phillip loosened all the horses and tied their reins to the saddle horns. A slap on their rumps sent them on their way home. Phillip jumped up behind Ben on Comanche.

As they rode away, Ben looked back at the confused men. Wes was roaring with laughter.

Chapter 13

When Ben, Phillip, and Wes rode up to the pasture gate, the door of the house flew open and the women of the two families crowded out to welcome them home. Fred came running from his cabin to tend the horses.

"Mr. Wes, Mr. Ben, thank de Lawd ya'll come home!"

Never had the three received so much hugging and kissing. Alice waited until last and kissed Ben full on the lips. Her mother and father smiled. The feel of her lips on his lingered with Ben all evening.

Blanche and the women had fixed a sumptuous meal, and soon all were seated around the big table. The men were ravenous and heaped their plates. As they ate, the rest talked. They had prayed the whole time the men were gone. Jack Farris had suggested that they fast and pray for the safety of the trio, and there had been sessions of scripture reading.

"Then Caroline had this experience. You tell it, Caroline," Jack said.

"Wes, I know that you don't hold to these things, but it really did happen." Caroline looked at Wes with brimming eyes. "I had been praying all day for you and the boys, and about two hours ago I was on my knees in our room and I heard a voice. Oh Wes, I really did! I was told, 'Prepare a feast, the men are coming home.' Oh, Wes, please believe me. It really did happen. See all this food we have prepared?" Tears were spilling down her cheeks now.

Wes rose from his seat and went around the table to Caroline, took her hands, and raised her to her feet. He held her a long time before speaking tenderly to her.

"I believe. . .I believe. In front of all these people I say it. I love you. I am now learning what real love is from you and Ben and these good people here. Don't expect perfection from me yet, but I am learning."

After the meal, when everyone was seated around the fireplace, Wes could wait no longer. His laughter rang out as he told of rescuing Phillip and of Ben's part in the affair.

"I was scooting up to the back of the store while Ben was diverting the attention of those buzzards. Phillip was in the back room all tied up. I had just made it quietly through the window to help Phillip, when I heard some talk about how cowardly I was, and Ben taking exception to what they said. Then I heard someone approaching from the outside. I left Phillip and sneaked up by the window, which I had left open for our escape. As a head appeared I laid my gun barrel on it, and the man just silently fell to the ground. By the time I had Phillip cut loose the noise had increased in the store, then the men all moved out in front of the building. Phillip and I climbed through the window and ran around the side just in time to see the fight start between Ben and Tom Jenkins. I was going to stop it, but Ben was doing so well I just stood back and watched. I had to hold on to Phillip. . . he was about to join the fight. I think those two would have whipped the whole bunch." Wes roared with laughter.

"Wes Bradford, you mean that you let Ben fight that grown man?" his wife rebuked him.

"Why stop a good thing? Jenkins had it coming! After all, Phillip was free, and we didn't have to shoot anyone. I'd say it was worth it, eh, Ben?"

Ben laughed. "You mean to tell me you stood there right from the beginning and watched? I guess I would have enjoyed it a little more if I had known you and Phillip were safe. Yeah...I guess I *did* enjoy it."

Phillip who had been quiet all evening spoke up, "I'll never have better friends than these two who were willing to chance being killed because of me. I heard the men in the store talk. They were really after Wes; they wanted to do him harm. If they could have gotten Ben at the same time that would have been all right with them, too. I thought you handled the situation very well."

"My family and I will always remember what you have done for us," Jack said. He started to get emotional, choked up, and could say no more.

Ben looked at Becky and Flo. Their eyes were misty as were all the others. Phillip had moved closer to Becky during the evening, and she had not moved away. Ben liked that. He let his mind wander to what the future could bring for them.

They all wanted to hear from Phillip about what had befallen him. It was as had already been surmised. He had been captured as the men had said. They had bound him and left him with a guard at the store. Then they took Ben's horse the long way around so the Mormons would not spot it. They were planning to get it close to home and turn it loose to frighten everyone and try to get Wes in a trap. The barn and White Stocking entered into their thinking and, Phillip supposed, that was what brought on the arson plan. He could hear them from the back room where he had been left, bragging about the fire. He thought that they had killed White Stocking. "Well," he said after giving his account, "I haven't had

89

much sleep, and neither have the rest of you." After Jack gave a prayer of thanksgiving for the safe return of the loved ones, all of them retired to bed.

Ben's thoughts were on Alice as he and Phillip retired to his room. He wondered what life held for them. He knew one thing, he wanted her in his life and he was going to do all in his power to keep it so. With that thought, he fell asleep.

The next few days were ones that Ben would long remember. Alice was near. A casual look sometimes brought a meeting of the eyes and a quick smile. There were rides about the countryside and touching of the hands. Neither set of parents said anything, but an occasional smile revealed their approval. Wes listened attentively as Jack told him of the angel visit to young Joseph Smith and the subsequent organization of the church, but he offered no comment. Phillip finally succeeded in getting Becky to talk to him, and they now seemed to have their own secrets. Caroline and Virginia helped Blanche in the kitchen and with the laundry and cleaning. Much of their conversation was about sewing and rearing children. Mischievous Flo tried all kinds of tricks to get attention—from heckling the two young couples, to talking her father into giving her a horse of her own.

Word reached them on the third day that was to upset again the serenity of the home. While Ben and Alice were riding they saw several men on horseback. A rider had stopped and was talking to Wes and Jack. The two men had their coats on, and Ben supposed that Wes had been pacing off where he wanted the barn built. He had been making plans for two days now. It was about time for the men to start rebuilding—that is, if they were going to show up.

Wes called him over as they dismounted and waved Alice on to the house. Ben watched her lithe stride as she moved quickly toward the porch and into the house.

"More trouble," Wes said.

Ben looked sharply at the visitor as he held the reins of the two horses. "What is it?"

Jack spoke. "It seems that the so-called militia took some of our men prisoners. Word got out that they planned to kill them. One of the brethren got a large group of Saints together and marched toward Independence. This frightened the townspeople. Colonel Thomas Wright sent a message to the Saints stating if they would surrender their arms they would be protected, and the men being held would not be harmed. There was talk back and forth, and the Saints finally surrendered fifty-one guns. Colonel Wright, knowing that the prisoners were being mistreated, took them to a cornfield and told them to leave. Of course, he had to have some recompense for his trouble, and one of the men gave him his watch to help defray the expense of keeping them in jail. The militia is going around the country now, driving our people from their homes in this cold weather and gathering them on the Temple Lot—a spot in Independence that is sacred to us. They are without shelter, and the so-called militia is riding around cursing and threatening them. There are women and children out in the cold. Now, it looks as if the weather is going to get really bad. I don't know what is going to happen next." Jack shook his head sadly.

The neighbor who had brought the news was in

sympathy with the Mormons. He reached down, picked up a twig, and with a pocket-knife fashioned himself a toothpick. He picked for a moment as his story sank in.

"Some of your people are down at the Wayne City Landing on the Missouri River waiting to be ferried across to the Clay County side," he went on with the story. "Boats all along the river are working. The people are camped up and down the bottoms waiting to get across. They say it is terrible. Some women are in the family way. They rushed them from their homes so fast that they have very little supplies. It's a shame. I have always said that." He chewed off a bit of the stick and spit it out of his mouth. "I guess I better be ridin'."

The men walked toward the house with long faces. The atmosphere inside was cheery and warm, but Ben did not feel it. Jack called his family to him and the rest gathered around. Phillip had been in the house with Ben's sisters playing a game and smiles were still on their faces as they joined the group; then they realized the seriousness of the gathering.

"What are we going to do, Papa?" Phillip asked.

"First of all, we have imposed on the Bradfords long enough. We are just making trouble for them now. It's time we took our place with the other Saints."

"Before a decision is made," Wes spoke up, "let me go to town and see how bad this is."

"I want to go with you," Ben said. "The rest ought to stay here until we look the situation over—right?"

"Right!"

Ben was astounded as they approached Independence. It was an armed camp with pitiful refugees gathered on the Temple Lot. Families were being driven in and their meager belongings dumped in the opening. Children were crying. Blankets had been thrown up in an attempt to protect them from the chilling wind that was steadily increasing in velocity. Campfires were here and there with weary people gathered around them. The militia had let some of the people go outside the perimeter to gather firewood. The militiamen were circling the camp, shouting insults. Most of them were drunk. It looked to Ben as if this was going to be a miserable night.

"I've seen enough, Ben. How about you?" Wes asked.

"I think we had better get back to the house. No telling what this bunch of riffraff will do to our friends if they come to our place. We ought to be there."

"Right, son."

Chapter 14

The ride home was a somber one. The mist was beginning to increase. Ben and Wes were silent, each alone in thought. When they arrived home they ate in silence, both sharing the same concern. The family that had seemed so happy a few days ago after the rescue of Phillip now seemed to be in mourning. The rain-softened turf had given them little warning that riders were approaching when Fred came running in without ceremony and cried, "Mr. Wes, looks like a hundred uv dem bad men comin' up de lane."

Wes jumped up from the table and grabbed his pistols. Running for the door, he yelled, "Everyone in the back bedroom."

Ben crowded the girls into the room. Jack and Phillip refused to go but stayed with Ben as he positioned himself at the front window with his rifle. Wes pulled a coat over his shoulders and stepped out onto the porch. The riders rode up into the yard and fanned out in front of the house. There were more than thirty.

Large pillars held up the roof of the porch, and Wes leaned against one of these. He held a pistol loosely in each hand—not threateningly, but where they could be plainly seen.

"What's going on?" he called out.

This was the militia—the protector of the down-trodden, the feeble. Were these men protecting the community from the dreaded Mormons—or the Mormons from the people? They were dressed in varied attire, but in a dashing captain's uniform at the head of

94

the group was Mr. McKeever, the storekeeper. Ben had forgotten that he had heard some time ago that McKeever had received such an assignment from the governor of the state of Missouri. Ben wondered why he had not participated more actively in the fracas at the store. Now he was the picture of confidence with all those men behind him.

The captain spoke. "Wesley Bradford, we have reason to believe that you are harboring a family of Mormons. We want them brought out immediately. They are to be interred at a camp provided for them until we can remove them from the county."

"I saw that camp, McKeever." Wes was not about to call him captain. "Would you want your family 'interred' there? If I had Mormons here, McKeever, you would be the last person I would turn them over to."

"Mr. Bradford," the captain said pompously, "We will not put up with any nonsense. I have over thirty men here, well-armed and skilled. I am their captain. If I give an order to open fire, you and all your household will be destroyed. This is a duly constituted militia of the state of Missouri. You must not interfere with the performance of our duty." He pulled himself up to his full height in the saddle.

Jack and Phillip headed for the door. Ben stopped them. "Wes can handle it. Watch him." Nevertheless he had his rifle ready.

Wes spoke so that all the men could hear. "Now you listen. I'm Wes Bradford. I want you to get that name straight. I've played cards with you. I've argued with you. We have had good times together. You know that I tell you true. If one man makes a move to carry out that order, I'm going to kill you and your leader. If I miss or get killed, Ben has a bead on you, and he has my orders to shoot to kill. Ben is on a rest, and I swear I have never seen him miss his mark on rest. I am going to get as many as I can of you before I die. McKeever, carry out your duty if you must."

The captain began to wheedle. "Now, Wes, we don't want trouble. We just want the people who are staying here. Tell them to come out and everything will be all right. We will treat them well. We just want them out of here. Some of them have already gone to Clay County."

"My offer still stands, McKeever. You are trespassing on my property and my time. Either you leave now or get shot. If I miss, Ben won't." Ben knew that Wes was mad clear through. His voice had that certain chill to it that he had always dreaded hearing while growing up. He knew if the shooting started he would have to carry out his part. He breathed a sigh of relief as he saw the men turn and start leaving the yard. McKeever's horse danced a little as he sensed the nervousness of his master who, looking around, saw that he was almost alone. Redfaced, he wheeled his mount and hurried to get at the head of his men who had turned toward Independence.

As Wes came in the house Ben gave a sigh of relief.

"What's the matter, Ben?" Wes laughed. "I wasn't going to shoot him...you were! My pistols weren't loaded." He laughed again. Ben didn't know if his father was joking or not. Wes's laughter brought the family out of the back room. When Caroline found out what happened, she grabbed Wes by the shoulders and shook him and shook him while he laughed at her.

96

Jack Farris spoke. "Wes, you and your wife have gone out of your way in protecting us. Enough is enough. My back has healed, and although I am a little stiff I'm able-bodied. We must leave today before we cause you any more trouble. Those men might be back. There is no point in your losing all you have—maybe even your life—because of us. Let's do it my way; I'll feel better about it."

"Jack Farris, you listen to me. I had more fun out there on the porch a while ago than you can imagine. Don't go and spoil it. I wouldn't have anything to fight over if you left."

Jack said with a smile, "I think you would find something. No . . . we must go."

"In the morning, then. We will hitch up the wagon and take you. "

Jack looked out the door at the weather, thought of his family, and said, "In the morning."

By night the rain had turned to sleet. Ben lay in his warm bed and thought of all the people camping in the open. His sleep was restless because he felt deeply the loss he was going to have with the leaving of his friends. Arising early, he found Phillip awake; they slipped quietly out to the pasture. He called up Comanche and caught another horse for Phillip. They saddled up, rode down the lane, and turned toward the Farris place. Ben shivered and turned his coat collar up. There was little to salvage when they reached what remained of the cabin. The women had already been over and picked up what they could. The boys did find one thing they were looking for, the ox yoke. After an hour's search they finally found the oxen in the brush. They herded the animals back to the remains of the cabin and yoked them up. Then they sat a long while looking at what had once been a home. Ben waited until Phillip wiped his eyes and turned his back on the scene. The two of them then drove the oxen to the Bradford farm.

The family was pleasantly surprised when the boys arrived with the oxen. Jack dashed out in his shirt sleeves and ran his hands lovingly over the animals. These would be sorely needed. He figured they had been stolen or shot. At breakfast Ben was seated next to Alice and Phillip next to Becky. Ben wondered if the girls had arranged the seating. Blanche had prepared hot biscuits, sausage, gravy, and a platter of fried eggs. Jack offered a prayer of thanksgiving for the food, for having had their lives spared, for the whole Bradford family, and for men like Ben and Wes—his voice broke. After a pause he said, "Amen." It was a solemn breakfast.

When the meal was over, each had a separate task to do before departure. Ben pulled Alice into the kitchen while Blanche was clearing the table. He held her in his arms and kissed her. With her arms about his neck, Alice responded. The kiss ended when Blanche entered with a tray of dishes, but it was a moment that both would long cherish.

They heard Jack call out, "Is everyone ready?" Alice loosened herself from Ben's embrace and ran to get her belongings. Ben felt empty. Here nice people were being removed from their homes for no other reason than their religious convictions. It was hard to believe that one group of people could be cruel to another group. Of course there was the matter of slaves. They had two, but they were never cruel to them. How was it going to end?

Chapter 15

Fred had hitched up the oxen to the wagon as Wes had ordered.

"Don't worry about returning the wagon," Wes had said. "We can pick it up later. You are not going very far. Better yet, keep it until you get settled and get your spring crop in. I have a hunch we will see you again after this blows over."

It was a tearful good-bye as Ben sat on Comanche waiting to escort the Farris family to the Wayne City Landing on the Missouri River. From there they would be ferried across to the Clay County side where the Saints were being welcomed. Everyone hugged everyone. Even Wes smiled through tear-filled eyes.

"You folks can depend on Ben," he told Jack. "He's the best."

"We know that," smiled Jack. "The law may never be straightened out so we can get our homes back, but I know one thing, we have met one fine family. God bless you and yours, Wes."

He shook Wes's hand again, and the oxen moved slowly down the lane and out onto the road. It was not far to the landing. After leaving Independence they found the road full of people straggling along afoot or with oxen or horses. It was very cold, and most of the people were poorly clothed. Little ones were crying. The militia rode among them, rifles across their saddles as if they expected trouble from this ragtag group of people who had given up everything but their faith in God.

The Farrises stopped and filled the wagon with as many people as it would hold. Before the trip was over,

Ben was leading Comanche so children could ride the buckskin. It was down hill after they went over the bluffs toward the river bottoms. On both sides of the river Ben could see the smoke of the campfires of the displaced persons. Ferries all up and down the river were working to get them and their meager belongings across to the Clay County side. They were just as glad to get across as the militia was to have them leave. Ben saw Captain McKeever, but the man gave him only a passing glance and moved on. Ben chuckled to himself. Unloading the passengers they had picked up along the way, the family made camp. Jack and Phillip went to find the one in charge to see when they could have their turn crossing the river. Ben helped the women with their tasks. That done, he took the oxen with a length of rope and started dragging up driftwood for a fire. In the meantime Jack and Phillip had returned with word that it would be tomorrow before they could cross.

Those with only what they wore and could carry were crossing the river in dugout boats. The militia men had taken their horses and cattle to "defray expenses of the militia" so they said. Many times, if they did not take the animals they shot them. One thing they did not mention was that mobbers made up most of the militia.

"Well, all we can do is wait," Jack said as they made a tent of the canvas Wes had sent along with the wagon. They looked around and saw many who were worse off than they were. Most of these people had weathered the rain and sleet of the night before. Two babies had been born there on the banks of the Missouri River. The crying of children was heard continually.

Wes and Caroline rode down in the late afternoon to

100

see about them. Blanche had sent a pan of bread and some fresh-churned butter with them, which was quickly devoured. Caroline and Wes had loaded the wagon with quite a bit of food for the Farrises to take across the river. (Before they could cross, however, they had shared it with the hungry about them.) Before dark Caroline and Wes said good-bye again, mounted, and rode for home.

The night was crisp and cold as the stars came out. Ben put more wood on the fire, and Alice left the tent which she was sharing with her parents. As she shivered from the cold, Ben opened his coat and wrapped it around her. Phillip was behind them in the wagon bed rolled up in a blanket for the night. Ben planned to join him there later.

"Alice," Ben spoke. "I know we are too young now, but someday we will be old enough to marry. I don't want anyone but you. You and your family and mine mean everything to me. I won't ask you to promise me now, but someday when things have straightened out I'm going to ride up to wherever you are. I'm going to take you by the hand and walk up to your father and say, 'Sir, I wish to marry your daughter.' He will say, 'What have you to offer?' I will say, 'Sir, only my love.' That *is* all I have to offer, Alice."

Ben felt the tears on Alice's cheek as she pressed her face against his. "That will be enough, Ben." She let him kiss her tenderly.

The spell was broken by the appearance of her mother as she came out of the tent and into the firelight. She said kindly, "Alice, it's time for you to come to bed."

"All right, Mama," Alice replied. "May I say good-night to Ben, first?"

"Don't be long."

"I won't, Mama."

The mother turned away and went into the tent. Ben held Alice close and gave her a lingering kiss. She pulled away reluctantly and was gone. Ben replenished the fire and crawled up into the wagon bed with Phillip. It was not too bad, for hay had been brought along for the oxen and Phillip had spread it out for them to sleep on. But sleep was far from Ben's mind. Eventually he drifted away dreaming of Alice.

Sometime in the early morning hours he was awakened by a loud cry in the camp: "Look at the heavens!"

The whole sky was filled with shooting stars. The tent flap opened; Alice, her mother, and father were sharply outlined by the light from the heavens. Thousands of meteors were blazing across the sky. Ben jumped down to stand close to Alice and hold her hand.

In astonishment Jack Farris said, "It is the handiwork of the Lord. He has not forgotten his people."

Someone began a hymn of praise. It was picked up by others until the whole camp was singing. Ben had never seen or heard anything like this. From that hour on the people of the camp were cheered. When the daylight arrived, they walked with joy in the midst of their trouble.

It was late afternoon before the Farrises and their possessions were taken across the river. Ben and Comanche were on the same boat load. The oxen were fresh and pulled the wagon out of the river bottom and onto the Liberty road. It was only a few minutes horseback ride to the little village of Liberty, but the oxen were slow. A kindly farmer allowed them and several other families to camp on his land. In spite of all that they had been through, there was a spirit of rejoicing as they built their campfires. Mush seemed to be the general fare for the evening meal, but there were few complaints.

Three days later, Ben was on the ferry crossing the Missouri River on his way home. He was the only passenger. On the north side of the river there were still some campers in makeshift shelters along the river bottom land. Help had come to the Saints, and while they still suffered, they were now among friends.

Jack Farris had found a teaching position and a little cabin for his family was part of his pay. Phillip had been hired by a contractor who was supplying wood for the steamboats that plied the Missouri River. The needy were being cared for by compassionate people who were willing to share what they had.

Ben had not left until he and Comanche brought back a deer for his friends. He had dressed it for them and hung it out of the reach of preying animals.

Jack had gone to his teaching tasks, and Phillip had gone to work. Only Virginia and Alice were in the cabin. When Ben was ready to leave, Virginia hugged and kissed him on the cheek. She turned her back on the young couple as she busied herself with a curtain for the one window of the cabin. Alice and Ben clung to each other for a long moment.

"I'll be back, Alice. It's not far. Remember what I said the night before the heavens were filled with shooting stars?"

"I remember," she answered.

He kissed her, and let his lips linger on hers. All too soon he had to open the door and close it behind him. Mounting Comanche, he headed for the river ferry. Yes, he would be back. The ferryman helped him on the ferry with his mount. As they were crossing the broad stream, the ferryman looked at him in wonder, for Ben, like Wes, turned his face heavenward and roared with the laughter of joy.

Postlude

A few years after the turn of the century, the descendants of these people returned to the "goodly land" of Jackson County and resettled. A large Auditorium now serves as the World Headquarters of their church—the Reorganized Church of Jesus Christ of Latter Day Saints. These people are making a valuable contribution to the community, the state of Missouri, and the world. They are respected. Their belief in a God who still speaks is no longer something to be feared as it was on the Missouri frontier in 1833. Saints now serve in all professions—science. . . medicine. . . sports. . . education. Some have served in various state governments and in the legislature of the United States.

A second group descended from those original settlers—the Church of Jesus Christ of Latter-day Saints with headquarters in Salt Lake City, Utah. Their industry and perseverance is a matter of history. They too have made valuable contributions to state and national government, and their people also make a fine contribution in the professional world. Although the name Mormon became commonplace through the years and ordinarily refers to these people affiliated with the Utah church, the word itself has a beautiful origin in a prophet who once lived in this land and organized the record of his people into a book of the testimony of the Lord's statement, "For God so loved the world that he gave his Only Begotten Son." This record is known as the Book of Mormon.